"Through humor, satire, and an uncanny knowledge of Latin American cultural nuances, Gordon Jackson has captured the essence of the debate over the purpose and value of short-term mission trips for both the receiving countries and the participants from the sending countries . . . It should be read by all mission committees, youth groups, and short-term teams at the beginning of their planning and training stages and would also be a valuable teaching tool in university courses on mission or missiology."

—DESIREE SEGURA-APRIL
Regional Missionary, United Methodist
General Board of Global Ministries

"To all coordinators of short-term mission teams, a warning: *Don't go on a cross-cultural mission trip until you've read this book!* Gordon Jackson's story includes almost every mistake, challenge, failure, and (by the providence of God) positive outcome that can be part of our well-intended but poorly prepared for efforts in short-term mission trips. The book will force you to evaluate your motivations, your training, and your team's readiness to serve."

—PAUL BORTHWICK
Senior Consultant, Development Associates International

"It's hard to imagine more things going wrong than what happened to the team headed to San Pedro! At the same time, it might have been the best thing that could have happened to this group. *The Mission Trip to San Pedro 2* provides a chance to think about what it means to receive as well as give, why we travel, and how we might think about service, wrapped in a page-turning story."

—BRIAN HOWELL
Professor of Anthropology and Coordinator of
Mission Studies, Wheaton College, Illinois

D0032433

"A hilarious and eye-opening look behind the scenes at a feel-good mission trip that goes horribly wrong. Or does it? Gordon Jackson strikes at the importance of getting international missions right and challenges the motives and methods of the sending church today."

—RANDY LARSEN
Recruitment and Mobilization, Engineering Ministries International

"This engaging story delivers a much-needed assessment of the inherent weaknesses of all too many churches' short-term mission efforts. But it also is a good reminder that our hosts are amazingly patient and gracious, Western church leaders' intentions are usually good, and people really can learn and improve. This book provides an entertaining way to open the eyes of short-term leaders to truths we all desperately need to understand."

—ELLEN LIVINGOOD
Founder and Director, Catalyst Services

"Gordon Jackson offers a timely challenge to the Western church in how they see and practice mission in the twenty-first century . . . This is a must-read for any local church missions board as they seek partnerships abroad to effectively bring gospel hope to communities rich in spirit, but poor in resources."

—ANDREW MERCER
Executive Manager, World Outreach International

"Gordon Jackson masterfully draws readers into the conversation around best practice regarding global missions and issues of international development. The irony and the humor will entertain you as you turn the pages, while serious dialogue and the arc of the story will make you consider the nuances and complexity of serving or working internationally."

—JOSH VINTON
Executive Director, Village Schools International

The Mission Trip to San Pedro 2

The Mission Trip
to San Pedro 2

Gordon S. Jackson

RESOURCE *Publications* · Eugene, Oregon

THE MISSION TRIP TO SAN PEDRO 2

Resource Publications
An Imprint of Wipf and Stock Publishers
199 W. 8th Ave., Suite 3
Eugene, OR 97401

www.wipfandstock.com

PAPERBACK ISBN: 978-1-6667-3184-2
HARDCOVER ISBN: 978-1-6667-2481-3
EBOOK ISBN: 978-1-6667-2482-0

10/12/21

In memory of Janeso

Contents

1

—

Departure

Saturday Morning

THE ENTIRE FIRST CHURCH group, to their credit, arrived at the Delta check-in area in ample time for their 7:20 departure. Moms, dads, and a smattering of sleep-deprived younger siblings were on hand to say goodbye to Ken, the youth pastor and group leader; the nine missioners; and Sissy Simons, the chaperone. Pastor Lawrence showed up too. Never a snappy dresser, he looked even more rumpled than usual; nor, it was obvious, had he shaved. But he was there to "wave the flag," as he put it, and gave a thoughtful prayer for the group's safety and spiritual growth during this venture.

The moms and dads gave their farewell hugs and last-minute words of redundant and obvious advice ("Now look after your passport," "Drink only bottled water, OK?" and "Be careful and don't do anything stupid . . ."). It was useful practice for dropping these same kids off at college one day, when similar admonitions flow freely, the parents not realizing that if their sons and daughters hadn't already embraced whatever last-minute wisdom mom and dad wanted to give them, it was too late now.

Ken had given them his own advice for the trip. He said that other than using their common sense, he identified four rules to ensure a positive experience for everyone:

- Don't be late for any commitments;

- Use the restroom whenever you have the chance, before things reach crisis proportions;

1

- No whining; and
- Look out for each other.

Kristen Sanker (one of the three Ks in the group: Kristen, Kyrstie and Kyra) stoically tried to hug away her mom's sobs, as almost all the rest of the group tactfully looked elsewhere. The lone exception was Kyra's four-year-old brother, Gary, who was intrigued by this grown woman openly crying, and crying hard, in a public place. As he pointed to Mrs. Sanker and began asking his mom a quintessentially honest and thus acutely embarrassing four-year-old type question, she yanked him away from the group.

Security went smoothly, mostly, and an adrenalin-driven laughing gaggle of First Church teens took their seats aboard the Delta flight. Sensitive to the hour, Ken moved around the cabin just before take-off, quietly telling the kids that on this whole journey they were serving as Christ's ambassadors, and that their fellow passengers would want quiet, not uproarious, unrelenting laughter during the three-hour flight ahead. Well, he put it more simply than that.

"OK?" he asked. Heads nodded. Then he reminded them of the importance of keeping regular journal entries. Ken resumed his seat next to Sissy and took out his slim trip binder. He glanced at his notes on the applications of the nine students accompanying him, wondering what this week held in store for them as individuals and as a group. Nine high schoolers: all juniors or seniors. And all white.

- Heidi Borgvik: Age seventeen. Passionate about kids; volunteered to plan the VBS and arranged the puppets. Wants to go into children's ministry.

- Annabel Burger: Kind, gentle, poised. Age seventeen. Especially mature for her age. Considering full time mission work after college. No clear college plans yet.

- Zach Estes: Just turned eighteen; oldest in the group. Self-assured, even cocky at times. A veneer for a deeper insecurity? But a natural leader.

- Bill Harris: Age seventeen. Keen athlete. Gregarious, friendly. Takes initiative on occasion but not a leader. Only limited interest in college but feels pressured by family to apply. No clear career goals.

- Kyra Johnson: Age seventeen. Mischievous sense of humor. Could be the group clown or prankster. But also highly empathetic. Diabetic. Keep close eye on her health.

- Tim McShay: The intellectual in the group. Age seventeen. Already applied to and admitted to three colleges. Wants to study physics. Thinks deeply about his faith; often asks probing (skeptical?) questions.

- Kyrstie Nichol: Age seventeen; stunningly attractive and knows it, without exploiting it. A guy magnet; but poised and able to handle the attention. Smart too. May need to keep a protective eye on her in San Pedro. No college plans at this stage.

- Kristen Sanker: Age sixteen; youngest in the group. Somewhat immature but with a good heart. A follower, not a leader. Need to keep a close eye on her.

- Sharon Ventry: Quiet, somewhat timid but has a deep faith. Serious about her Christian discipleship. Age seventeen. A strong soccer player despite her diminutive size. Looking at attending the local community college.

Seated next to him, Sissy was even more tense than usual; her plan of knitting during today's flights was thwarted when a TSA official confiscated her needles. Her protest to the official that she was on a missionary trip got her nowhere. To assuage her disgruntlement and to forestall what Ken expected might be a long and unwelcome conversation to relieve her anxiety, he rather flippantly suggested she read her Bible. She earnestly took up his suggestion and Ken put on his eye-mask and drifted into his second light sleep that day.

2

———

Earlier that Morning

KENDALL BARKER'S THEOLOGY DIDN'T allow him to believe in omens. But with departure now less than seven hours away he was unsettled and, as a result, struggling to sleep. It wasn't just nervousness over leading his first mission trip. He sensed it was something more. He feared that the three events of the past week added up to more than just a sum of their parts. But he found himself struggling to do the math.

First, there was the failure of Jerry Binder to come through with his pledge of $1,500 to help underwrite the trip. Despite repeated requests for his check, Jerry didn't deliver. This meant the group was now about $2,200 under budget. Pastor Lawrence had earlier assured Ken that the church would find the funds to cover a $700 shortfall. But Jerry's non-payment moved things to a different level. With a Saturday morning departure already set, and with all the other arrangements in place, they'd have to go ahead and make up the shortfall later.

Neither Ken nor Pastor Lawrence had been at First Church long enough to know this wasn't the first time Jerry Binder had overpromised support for church projects. Yes, the trip would go ahead, but Ken was angry and disappointed that the group would return from their venture knowing they'd have to take yet another shot at fundraising. Ken and the pastor agreed to keep the business about Jerry's non-payment to themselves, to avoid casting any shadow over the trip.

The second blow, however, was impossible to hide. On Tuesday, Irma Watson pulled out of the trip. Her aging mother had a major heart attack and Irma left immediately to be with her in Nebraska. Understandable, of course, but still a body blow to Ken. He was counting more than he'd care to admit on Irma's maturity, wisdom and experience on at least half a dozen similar mission trips. Now he had only one chaperone: Sissy Simons. Christian charity compelled Ken to accept Sissy's eager offer to serve as an "under-chaperone," as she put it.

"Christian charity compelled . . ." was a phrase associated with Sissy Simons more often than not. She was not Ken's favorite person at First Church; indeed, she was probably nobody's favorite person at First Church. In her late twenties, Ken saw her as insecure, always on the defensive. While there was no doubting the depth of her faith, it apparently didn't translate into any joy in her life. Sissy was not, in other words, an easy person. Ken's hesitations about her joining the team were overridden by his expectation of Irma's presence. Always sensible and saintly, Irma assured Ken that with a little direction and encouragement, Sissy would not be a problem on what was her first mission trip. Now, with Irma gone, Ken feared that in addition to all his other responsibilities, he'd have to add to his duties chaperoning the sole remaining chaperone.

Also on Tuesday the travel agent called to say that Delta had rescheduled one of their flights. The itinerary was the same but their connection through Atlanta was now considerably tighter: only forty-seven minutes. Although an optimist by nature, Ken began to think of all the things that could go wrong. What if they arrived in Atlanta just fifteen minutes late? Would that give them time to make their way to a distant gate in the nation's busiest airport? And what about the bathroom breaks? For reasons he'd never determined, teenage girls (who apparently learned this behavior from their mothers) needed to visit restrooms in clusters—and spend far more time doing whatever they did than teenage boys. The group, apart from Sissy and himself, consisted of nine teens: six girls and three boys. The bathroom issue loomed larger the more he thought about it.

Then his thoughts shifted, as he realized that even if they made it to their flight, their checked luggage might not. That could be a major headache. The packing list and instructions he and Irma gave the group clearly anticipated a lost-luggage scenario: Make sure your carry-on luggage includes several days' changes of clothing, your toiletries, and any meds you need. Other clothing plus the Vacation Bible School supplies were destined for checked luggage, as were the four suitcases of gently used children's clothing for distribution in San Pedro.

As he lay awake at 2:30, Ken's head swirled with all these pieces. It was as if he were watching a slow-speed blender, with chunks of potential trouble appearing in front of him, then moving on to be replaced by other chunks. An organized person, Ken kept telling himself: "I've done everything I know to prepare for the trip." He then committed the trip yet one more time to God: "Lord, I know you're in charge of this. Please forgive me and help me to overcome my doubts and anxieties."

Especially because this was his first mission trip, either as a participant or a leader, Ken was meticulous in thinking through the arrangements. He and Irma took care of everything, including detailed packing lists and instructions for the high-schoolers ("don't bring your phone—you won't be able to use it"); to arranging their activities on site in San Pedro; and liability waivers. First Church had no recent experience with any mission teams going outside the country. Ken's predecessor as the church's youth pastor had for each of the four summers prior to Ken's arrival led high school groups on the same inner-city service project in Denver. Now, in his second year as youth pastor, Ken wanted to do something bolder and give the youth group exposure to ministry outside their comfort zone—an idea that Pastor Lawrence and the church leadership enthusiastically supported.

His desire to do something international, and his own inexperience in this area, led him and Irma to work with an agency she knew from the mission trips she had done before joining First Church two years ago. The agency, Mission Matchers Inc., was highly regarded, Irma said. The agency matched you with a "receiving" church carefully screened for various factors. These included the receiving organization's specific needs, interests of the sending church or parachurch group, theological compatibility, and availability of a skilled "host" or point person with conversational English proficiency. The receiving organization undertook to provide accommodation and feed the incoming mission team.

Ken and Irma had, with Mission Matchers' help, settled on working with a small church in the village of San Pedro. The village, with a population of about 400, was a ninety-minute drive from San Gabriel, the town into which they would fly. The team would paint the church and run a Vacation Bible School from Monday through Friday. Mission Matchers arranged to buy the supplies the team would need in San Pedro and reimburse the local hosts for the week's room and board.

The plan: arrive early evening on Saturday and conduct the worship service on Sunday, translation to be provided by Ricardo, their "host" or point person, with whom Irma and Ken had held several spotty but still useful Zoom conversations. In their most recent conversation, on Monday, Ricardo assured them that the funds from Mission Matchers had come through and allowed him to buy paint and other supplies, which he had already delivered. Even though the Zoom images of Ricardo were always grainy, Ken was comforted in knowing who to look for on their arrival.

As he thought of that last conversation with Ricardo, he felt more relaxed. No, he didn't believe in omens. His breathing eased and the chunks in his mind's blender began to blur and fade. It was close to 3 a.m. when Ken finally drifted into a much-delayed and tentative sleep that ended with the alarm telling him it was 5:15—and time to get ready for the airport.

3

—

Ricardo Doesn't Show

Saturday Evening

KEN'S FEARS ABOUT THE connection in Atlanta were partly justified. Their plane landed on time but they had to wait nearly fifteen minutes before they could get to their gate. The pilot's occasional apologies for the delay did nothing to quell Ken's rising anxiety. Fortunately, their connecting flight was only three gates away and with boarding passes in hand they made it with a few minutes to spare. So concerned was he about getting himself and the ten others on board that he didn't consciously consider that their checked luggage was now destined for an extended stay in Atlanta.

Thankful to have made the connection, Ken put on his eye mask once again as they left Atlanta and for the first time that day fell into a deep, sound sleep. He slept equally well on the leg from Miami, until Sissy shook him awake. He barely had time to complete the immigration form the flight attendant had left for him before they landed in a heavy rain.

Next came immigration: A cheery officer looked at Ken's passport picture, at him, and the ten others in what was obviously his entourage. Confirming Ken's purpose of visit as "tourism," he chuckled and said, "Ah, mission trip." Then he flipped through the pristine passport but when he got to the back he frowned. He said gravely, "Not valid."

"What?" Ken said.

"Must sign," the official replied, with a grin, pointing to the signature space Ken had never even noticed. "Not valid until signed."

Having pointed out to Ken at least one detail he had not attended to, the official stamped the passport with the practiced insouciance of official-dom. But before sliding it back to him under the glass partition separating them he asked, "So you are here for mission work, yes?"

Ken responded awkwardly, as if his mom had rightfully accused him of taking those last cookies. "Er, yes. For one week."

"Where will you be going?" It seemed to be asked out of mere curios-ity but Ken couldn't be sure. He knew to answer honestly.

"San Pedro."

"And you are working with a mission organization here?"

"Yes," said Ken. "Mission Matchers."

"Good, good," the official said. He knew the organization.

He then concluded their exchange by saying, "Welcome, welcome to Santa Gabriella." He returned the passport and waved Ken through.

The official perfunctorily processed the rest of the group, asking no questions to corroborate Ken's story, and they soon rejoined him.

The "welcome to Santa Gabriella" vaguely triggered something in Ken's mind but he was right now so focused on getting their luggage that it didn't quite register.

Ken found an ATM and using his debit card, withdrew a small amount of cash; Ricardo recommended that he have a modest amount of local cur-rency on hand. Then he led the way to luggage claim. Only then did it hit him: There almost certainly had not been enough time in Atlanta for their bags to join them. He was right. Twenty minutes later the carousel finally ceased its mindless, empty rotations. Ken told the group they'd have to re-port their delayed luggage once they went through customs.

"What about the puppets?" cried Heidi, who was the self-appointed leader of this aspect of the VBS program. She and others had put in enor-mous effort making special "multicultural puppets for Jesus," following pat-terns they'd discovered on the web. The website promised that the puppets were endearing to children of any culture. How valid a claim that was, Ken didn't know. For now, the puppets would have to enjoy each other's com-pany while they were stuck in Atlanta; Ken had other concerns.

Ken found the local Delta agent and lined up the group to describe their bags and show their luggage tags. Ken went first, he said, because he wanted to connect as soon as possible with Ricardo.

By now only a handful of people remained in the arrival area for friends or relatives. Ken thought none of them looked like Ricardo. He was right; none of them was. Fending off three offers from taxi drivers who all assured him of a good price and a clean vehicle, he went out to the curb to see if Ricardo was there. No sign of him. More taxi drivers sought his custom. He got out his phone and notebook. He looked up the number Ricardo gave him in their last Zoom chat but on dialing got what for him was an unintelligible recorded message in Spanish. He tried again. Same message. He checked the number: yes, he had it right. But this time, he couldn't get a signal.

Then he remembered what Mission Matchers called a troubleshooting number. He found it in his notebook, momentarily taking pride in how proactive he had been. But then he found that he still couldn't get a signal. He assembled the group, which was complete except for Sissy and Kyrstie. "They're in the bathroom," someone said.

Ken was tempted to be irritated over how long it was taking them when he realized they weren't exactly in a hurry. Kyrstie and Sissy appeared, with the younger of the two wearing an expression that clearly said, "Not my fault—but I had to stay with her." She whispered to Ken, when she got close enough, "She was putting on her makeup. Go figure."

It was now just after 7:30; Ricardo had said he would be in the arrivals area by 7, in case their flight arrived early. And he'd have two ten-seater vans, more seats than they needed but with ample room of the luggage—which Ricardo had now apparently also joined on a no-show list.

Ken's movements of looking hopefully at all arriving vehicles and frequently looking at his watch signaled that he was an increasingly promising target for the few remaining taxi drivers who had not yet secured fares for the evening. At about two-minute intervals they'd take turns pestering him with their mantra reserved for obvious foreigners: "Cheap price, clean car."

He called the group together. "Listen folks, I don't know what's happened," he said. "But our man isn't here yet. I guess we'll just have to wait."

Zach, the biggest of the three teen boys and someone who appeared to be perpetually hungry, predictably asked what others no doubt were beginning to think: "Hey, can we get something to eat?"

Not having noticed any restaurants or fast-food places on his walk through the airport, Ken was dubious. He was also reluctant to have them scatter, in case Ricardo arrived. But he couldn't ignore a need that, admittedly, he too was beginning to feel. Hence, a compromise: He said, "Zach, go and check out the place and see if you can find anything. Don't buy anything—just find out what options we have. If Ricardo arrives soon, maybe we can get some quick take-aways or supplies on the way." He added, "Be back in five minutes."

Zach nodded and took off. Seven minutes later he was back, shaking his head. "Nothing," he reported. "Everything's shut."

Ken was formulating two plans. First, he'd decided that if Ricardo hadn't shown by 8:30, he'd have to give in to the persistent taxi drivers and hire two of them to get them to San Pedro before it was much later. Second, food. He realized his generous supply of power bars and other snacks was in his checked luggage, but he had a couple of Clif bars and some trail mix. In what was something of a re-enactment of the feeding of the five thousand, he asked what the others had to share. Not much emerged, mostly the kind of junk food that Jesus would no doubt have had some hesitation multiplying for the masses. But it was enough, for now anyway; everyone got a bit to tide them over.

Ken sent Zach on another mission: "Go and check if there are more flights arriving tonight. These taxi drivers are going to head out after the last flight and we'd be stuck if Ricardo still doesn't show." Zach reappeared with what Ken supposed was good news. The last flight of the evening came in just after 9. At least that bought them more time to use the taxis, if they needed them.

And so they waited. Ken tried his phone again but still no signal. His battery looked good and while earlier he had got four bars his reception was now down to one. Maybe, he thought, as cynicism and frustration began to take hold, just maybe everything in this country shuts down at sunset. When 8:15 arrived and Ricardo didn't, Ken began to look more carefully at his remaining taxi options. It might be a squeeze but he thought they could fit all eleven of them into two of the bigger cars still waiting to be filled. By now, the rain was coming down harder.

4

——

Ken Takes the Initiative

Saturday Evening

TRYING TO BE CHARITABLE, Ken wanted to believe that something beyond Ricardo's control had occurred. A flat tire or a mechanical problem with his van. An accident perhaps? Or maybe he was ill. But if he couldn't make it, why was the other driver also missing? No, he concluded reluctantly, the more likely explanation was "Third World Syndrome"—where you just couldn't expect the reliability that one assumed, and demanded, in the developed world.

Still striving to be charitable, Ken assumed that at least in Ricardo's mind there'd be a valid reason for not showing up. Who knows, maybe the baby-sitter let him down, or he had to take a neighbor to hospital. Yes, he was frustrated on behalf of the group that they'd barely arrived in the country and already his planning was falling to pieces. But just as troubling was that Ricardo, who had sounded so organized in their Zoom chats, had now proven to be so unreliable.

He expected that when they eventually connected, Ricardo would overflow with apologies for an excuse that quite frankly wouldn't wash back home. Well, he'd deal with that when the moment arose. Or *if* the moment arose; it was evident that Ricardo wasn't about to appear this evening.

At 8:30 Ken relented. He approached the nearest taxi driver and said, "*San Pedro—once personas.*" The man laughed and shook his head. He spoke rapidly in Spanish. Ken understood not a word but clearly, and correctly, got the message: "If you think I'm going to drive all the way to San Pedro in this weather, you're nuts."

But then the man reconsidered and gestured to Ken that he should wait, as if he had an alternative. He went off and talked with another of the drivers and the two men approached him.

"*Americano?*" the first driver asked.

"*Sí*," said Ken, using about another 20 percent of his Spanish vocabulary. He knew this admission would increase any fare probably threefold. But he could hardly hide his and the group's all-too-obvious gringo status.

"*Fifty dollars para mi,*" said the man, and turning to his colleague added, "*Y fifty dollars para mi amigo.*"

Ken engaged halfheartedly in some bargaining, all too aware of his disadvantage. Finally they agreed on forty apiece and Ken gestured to everyone to get into the two vehicles. To his surprise, the one he got in lived up to the driver's promise of being clean. It also was in relatively good shape, except for the windshield wipers that did perpetual but never quite effective battle against the rain.

Ken was in the front seat of the front car. With him were Zach and three others in the back: Tim, Bill and Heidi. It was tight but not intolerable. The car behind them had Sissy in the front seat. Her unhappiness over how the rain must have messed up her makeup was overtaken by her anxiety over how closely the driver followed his colleague, the volume of the car radio, and his odd way of repeatedly looking at her and asking, "San Pedro?" And on getting no answer but a nod of the head, would ask again in two or three minutes, "San Pedro?"

Next to her was the smallest of the girls, Sharon, sharing one seat belt of dubious cleanliness. Behind her were a very cramped quartet: the "three Ks," Kristen, Kyrstie, and Kyra, plus Annabel. Fortunately, this was the larger vehicle, an old but seemingly immortal Mercedes. They had tried in vain to sort out the three tangled seatbelts before turning to shrugs and silent prayer.

⚬⊱⚬

As they drove in silence in the dark, Ken saw the journey as a metaphor of his entry into ministry. He grew up in a Christian home and while his faith was always an integral part of his life, it was only when he was a junior in high school—the same age as most of the kids in the group—that he made what he now regarded as a genuine commitment to Christ. He majored in biology in college, with no particular career goal in mind. But the mentorship by the leader of the campus ministry led him to consider more and more the possibility of full-time ministry.

Then, in his senior year, still unclear what lay ahead after graduation, the call came. In a powerful and impossible-to-explain encounter in his dorm room, he read for the umpteenth time the words of Isaiah, in chapter six: "Here am I. Send me." Two things struck him about Isaiah's experience. The first was the prophet's unswerving, unhesitating answer to God's question, "Whom shall I send? And who will go for us?" He too felt compelled to commit fully, right then, to God's service.

The second thing was how Isaiah said "send me" without the slightest idea where he was to go or what he was to do. Ken felt the same. He had no sense of *what* God was calling him to do, at least, not yet. But he knew for a certainty that his calling was real; God would fill in the details later.

Upon graduating he still had no clarity on the specifics of his call. The road, like the one to San Pedro, was dark. He prayed for light to illuminate his path. And he prayed. And he prayed. Nothing. But he knew he couldn't sit idle. Fortunately, he was able through someone his dad knew to get a job working in a law firm. His liberal arts degree equipped him well and the work was initially interesting. But after three years, when his learning curve had flattened, the work became tedious and lacked its initial challenge.

Then things suddenly fell into place. It's been said that God may seem slow but he's never late. God's timing in Ken's life consisted of three developments, in quick succession. First, he experienced a simultaneous sense that his time at the law firm was ending and that the time was ripe to begin training for full-time ministry. Second, he had what seemed like a chance meeting with his college ministry mentor, Karl Michaels. He impressed on Ken the option of going to seminary, suggesting one that he thought was a good match. So he applied. The third, and clinching, element was the seminary's prompt offer of admission. The offer came with a full tuition waiver for the three-year program, thanks to a generous endowment built over 230 years.

His call to the youth pastor role at First Church was his first out of seminary. It was a good match, he thought. Theologically, he was on the same page as the pastor and, from what he could tell in the interview process, with the church council as well.

Pastor Lawrence was supportive and mostly let Ken "do his thing," as he put it, while always being accessible when Ken needed advice. The church community too was supportive. Well, mostly. He had several run-ins with Heidi's father, Andre Borgvik. Pastor Lawrence warned him that the man was hyper-protective of his daughter and that Ken should humor him as much as possible but stand his ground when necessary.

Pastor Lawrence gave Ken occasional preaching opportunities, which Ken enjoyed. But mostly his mandate was to strengthen the already vibrant youth program, especially the teens. The church council and the pastor agreed this was the group that was most likely to fade away from their faith unless they were deeply grounded. It was Ken's job to ensure that they were.

The San Pedro mission trip was one element to advance that goal. With Irma's help, he selected the ten students whom they thought would benefit most from the San Pedro trip. They rejected two applicants, both of whom Ken and Irma thought were too immature to handle the rigors of the trip. One of them had come to him in tears after getting the rejection. The tears soon gave way to a rant about how unfair Ken and Irma were in rejecting her when all her youth group friends were accepted and everyone would think she was a loser and how unfair this was and how they rejected her because her parents weren't members of the church and how unfair this was. The rant, combined with the fact that she brought her mother with her, simply confirmed the wisdom of Ken and Irma's initial decision. (The mom said only, "I think it's just so unchristian, so unchristian.")

They had accepted a tenth student but he dropped out because he got mono.

So here he was, with the remaining nine, plus a chaperone, on a dark road in unknown territory, in heavy rain, and without the guide who should have met them. Ken was in a sense traveling blind tonight, thinking again how that paralleled his own faith journey in which God had shown him only one step at a time.

He was reminded of those words that were pivotal to his call when he was finishing up in college: "Here am I—send me." Now, with the uncertainty because of Ricardo's absence, he prayed, "Lord, I'm concerned that something's wrong. Please help me to trust you; give me your wisdom to know what to do." He believed that God had gone before them and was even now preparing their way. He hoped that way would be clearly marked with God's light. And that if Ricardo didn't show, that God would make clear the guidance they needed for this uncertain road ahead.

☙

Ken knew from his conversations with Ricardo that San Pedro was a ninety-minute drive from the airport. He was taken aback when they arrived at a mostly darkened village after about fifty minutes, and his driver (whose name by now he had learned was Carlos) slowed and announced, "San Pedro."

The rain had eased but the darkness made it difficult to make out any of the village's features. He had somehow conveyed to Carlos that they were going to the community's lone church. Carlos pulled up next to some men smoking under the awning outside a small café. He asked them, so Ken assumed, where the church was. The men appeared puzzled. Then, simultaneously, two of them pointed in opposite directions. Some intense chatter followed. Carlos turned to Ken and said, "*Hay dos iglesias: católica y evangélica.*"

Two churches? That much he understood. This didn't make sense. Mission Matchers' information was absolutely clear: San Pedro had only one church.

Something was wrong. Ken's exhausted mind couldn't begin to think what it was. But he was still alert enough to recall his reflection last night about omens.

5

Arrival

Saturday Evening

KEN TOLD CARLOS, "EVANGELICAL." The driver nodded and engaged in another burst of conversation with the men outside the café. Ken understood none of it but correctly inferred that directions were forthcoming.

Carlos pointed enthusiastically ahead and said yet more fast and, to Ken, unintelligible Spanish. They drove on through the rain, with Ken peering through the windshield and rain for anything that resembled a church. Suddenly Carlos turned left, with the Mercedes close behind, onto what was obviously an unpaved, rutted road—judging from the sudden bounces. After about thirty or forty yards, Carlos stopped and pointed triumphantly at a single-story concrete building, with a corrugated iron roof and a double door at the front, one half of which opened onto a dim light inside.

"*Iglesia!*" Carlos proclaimed, as if he had found the Holy Grail itself. Ken's reaction was a mix of gratitude at having found *a* church, plus puzzlement because it was clearly not the one he'd seen in the photos Mission Matchers had sent. Still, knowing this was his best bet—indeed, his *only* bet—right now, he told his back-seat crew, "Wait here until I can find out what's going on." He got out, walked to the Mercedes, and rapped on Sissy's window. He told her the same thing.

Ken tentatively approached the door. Inside, seated in a circle near the door were five women, all in their fifties or sixties, he concluded from a quick glance. With their heads bowed, none of them noticed him.

He was loath to interrupt a prayer meeting, especially when he wasn't even sure what he would tell these people. But he knew too that he couldn't stand there indefinitely.

In his residual high school Spanish, he said, "*Buenas dias.*" The women looked up, surprised but not alarmed at this rain-spattered, dog-tired and obviously confused stranger.

"*Buenas noches,*" one of them corrected him in her response. Her voice was soft but authoritative. The woman was, as Ken had surmised, probably in her mid-fifties. Her face had a roundness that matched the chubbiness of her body. Her hair was mostly gray and neatly platted. But it was her eyes that Ken found arresting: They were at the same time searching and remarkably gentle.

Ken suspected he'd made eye contact with her longer than was culturally appropriate, before he asked, "*Habla Ingles?*"

The woman responded, "*Si, un poco*—little bit."

The woman to her left added, "Yes, please?"

Then began a tortuous conversation, pieced together over what seemed like ages, as Ken tried to explain in fragments of Spanish and the women tried to respond in similar fragments of English the who, what, why, and how of Ken's plight. The "where" was all too obvious; there they were altogether in this place, all of them trying to figure out what God expected of them next.

Carlos entered the building and interrupted to get Ken's attention and pointed vigorously first to his watch and then out the door. The message was clear. Carlos and his fellow driver wanted to head home. Carlos greeted the women with obvious respect, and they engaged in a brief but earnest and energized conversation. Ken gathered that Carlos was making some kind of pitch to them and the women agreed. Then they said a few things to themselves, before saying what sounded like a conclusive statement to Carlos, who in turn nodded in agreement.

He turned to Ken and said, "You stay here, *si*? Come." He took Ken's shirt sleeve and gently pulled him outside, toward the car. The message was clear: this unknown church, in this unknown place, with these unknown women, was to be their next stop on their improvised itinerary.

Ken told everyone to bring their hand luggage and go into the church. He then dug into his wallet to find some twenties. He found only a few tens and some fifties, so he just gave Carlos and his buddy (whose name he never learned) each a fifty, shook their hands, and then scurried out of the rain once more into the shelter of the church.

If he hadn't been so tired, he might have laughed at the scene. To one side was his flock: Nine young Americans and a chaperone stood in a state of collective bewilderment, assuaged ever so slightly by the reality that they had at least arrived *somewhere*. Even though they didn't know where they were or what they were doing, their apprehension was eased too at having found shelter in a church. Spartan though it was, this simple structure dedicated to God was for these beleaguered travelers a sanctuary.

To the other side stood the group's suddenly acquired hosts. They talked quietly but animatedly among themselves, with gestures seemingly punctuating every thought. As Ken re-entered the building he heard one of the women saying, "*Ovejas perdidas!*—Lost sheep!" As if on cue, all five women laughed. Acknowledging the aptness of the description, the First Church group laughed just as heartily in response, desperately needing a catharsis. The laughter wasn't enough of a release for Sharon, however. In a matter of moments, her laughter metamorphosed into tears, which came slowly at first, then uncontrollably.

The kindly-eyed woman quickly moved beside her and held her tightly, as if she was simultaneously holding the girl together while squeezing out her sobs. With her right hand she gently rubbed her back and began singing softly.

As the others looked on with a mix of fatigue, discomfort and gratitude to be *somewhere*, Ken still had no idea where he had brought them. But he knew this was a good place.

6

Ricardo Perplexed

Saturday Evening

RICARDO WAITED AT THE airport until 9, even though the sleepy guard at the main security gate assured him that no more incoming flights were scheduled—which Ricardo dutifully confirmed with a more alert functionary at Delta's luggage claim office. "Any possibility that they may have been transferred to another flight?" Ricardo asked.

"No, no more flights due in tonight; just one commuter flight is heading out in twenty minutes, to San Jose."

Ricardo had planned to spend the night at Pastor Sanchez's home, along with Ken and one of the boys. Instead, he let the pastor know of the group's non-arrival. Neither of the men could account for the group's absence, despite a flurry of phone calls and texts, including to Mission Matchers, Pastor Lawrence back at First Church, and the nearest Delta office.

Ricardo was the model of tact and calm when he reached Pastor Lawrence; while he admitted he did not know where the group could be, he told the pastor not to worry. Several groups he had worked with in the past had been delayed or re-routed, he said; and even though nobody knew what could have happened to the group he was certain they'd arrive the next morning—and he'd be back at the airport to greet them.

Pastor Lawrence's response registered somewhere between puzzlement and worry, but he took Ricardo at his word that the group would appear soon—probably with some perfectly understandable explanation for their initial non-arrival. Ricardo assured him that he'd contact him early the next morning, before church, to update him.

Ricardo, realizing there was nothing more he could do, found a hotel close to the airport that was inexpensive but still respectable enough for a representative of Mission Matchers, where he and his fellow driver checked in for the night.

7

Getting Re-Oriented

Sunday Morning

KEN AWOKE AT 6:33 to clattering sounds coming from the kitchen and to the smells emanating from the same source. He thought he could identify eggs; he couldn't tell what else was being prepared. The prospect of food reminded him how hungry he was and his mind did an instant replay of the developments that had brought him to this bed, in this village.

Sharon's meltdown the previous night, he now recalled, ended soon enough. The woman comforting her (whose name Ken later learned was Ana) somehow explained that the group was to be divided among the five women, and a few friends. Through gestures, the women conveyed that although their homes were small, the group would spend the night there. The next morning, as Ken understood it, someone who spoke good English would arrive and take things from there.

So, as he entrusted the nine youth group members and Sissy into the care of complete strangers, he saw his carefully crafted mission trip taking an utterly unanticipated direction. Ana, however, exuded such an air of "in-chargeness" that he surprised himself by how easily he accepted the situation. Of course, he asked himself as the group dispersed, what choice did he have? It's not as if this small village provided a range of options between a Four Seasons and a Motel 6. He was intensely grateful that these gracious women were doing what he could not: take care of his small flock.

As the group split up, Ken tried reassuring them that everything was OK. For the most part, the group embraced a spirit of adventuring into the unknown. He thought that Sissy, not surprisingly, looked most anxious. But he could tell she was putting on a brave face while completely out of her element.

For Sissy didn't relax easily, or often. Raised as an only child by severe parents, who attended an equally severe church, Sissy was conditioned from her earliest days to regard faith and fear as inextricably linked. Her parents, loving though they were, instilled in her the conviction that people's souls walked a knife-edge between perdition and pardon for their sins. Not surprisingly, she came to see God as much like her parents: a severe being whose love was merited only by avoiding wrong-doing. The faith she acquired was thus marinated in guilt and devoid of joy. Her church leaders would have disavowed H. L. Mencken's definition of puritanism as "the haunting fear that someone, somewhere, may be happy." In reality, though, that was the ambiance in which Sissy was raised.

After graduating from high school she wanted to attend college, although she didn't have any particular academic direction. Her parents desperately wanted her to attend a nearby Christian college, where she'd be safe from the secular world, but couldn't afford the tuition. Instead, she enrolled at a state university. Supported by unrelenting prayers, by her mother in particular, for her physical and spiritual safety, Sissy embarked on a satisfactory but undistinguished academic career.

She majored in history, with a minor in Spanish. Ideally, she would have loved to major in theater, to which she'd been secretly drawn since she saw a stunning performance in her high school of *Fiddler on the Roof*. She fantasized what it would have been like to be part of that cast, especially since the production was a musical that would have allowed her to engage in one of her few parentally-approved activities and sources of fulfillment: singing. But she knew that her parents would never have tolerated her cozying up to that "cesspool of temptation" that her dad associated with the world of theatre. Avoiding the sciences, and its atheistic propagandists, was also a given. (Sissy's parents were devout six-day creationists; Sissy increasingly had her doubts on this matter, which she wisely refrained from sharing.)

So history it was. It was difficult for her parents to find strong objections to that choice. "All we do is look at what's already happened," Sissy would explain. "It's not like political science where you get exposed to all those liberal ideas," she said. And that satisfied them.

After graduation Sissy was fortunate enough to find a job as an archivist with the state historical society. That entailed a move to another town, and of course a move to another church. Hence her affiliation with First Church. It could be described as a middle-of-the-road evangelical church, more tolerant by far than the one in which she was raised—which caused her parents, especially her mother, ongoing concern. Sissy's mission over Easter, Thanksgiving and Christmas family get-togethers was to keep assuring her parents that First Church was nothing like those liberal churches that didn't even deserve to be called "churches." No, First Church, she told them, was a good place for her.

And it was. The church served as something of an incubator for her, slowly bringing to fruition her spiritual maturity and social skills. Yes, she still bore the scars of guilt and defensiveness; those would never disappear completely. While she remained "Miss Awkward" in the eyes of many, including Ken, what hardly anyone at First Church realized was how much more mellow and mature she had become in the seven years she had been a member.

Invariably, the unfamiliar rattled her. So she was in high anxiety mode on her arrival in San Pedro, unsure of her role with this group of young people with whom she had nothing in common besides her faith. She had come on this trip because she felt increasingly convicted to take some steps to stretch her faith horizons. In her women's Bible study, someone had said Christians need to take "God-inspired risks." So she had.

Ken had gone with Ana, whom he concluded was a widow. Her concrete block house had two-bedrooms, a small dining area, and a small kitchen (about the size of a generous closet). The kitchen had its own exterior door, through which she took him by the hand a few steps into the rain to point him to the outhouse—about fifteen yards away. He nodded understandingly, grateful that his faithfully followed packing list included a flashlight. When they came back inside, she pointed to a blue plastic bowl at the kitchen sink and motioned hand-washing. Interestingly, he thought, the house had indoor plumbing, at least for cold water—but no indoor toilet. She gave him a one-liter bottle of water, gesturing that he shouldn't drink from the kitchen faucet, and a chipped but clean mug. He could brush his teeth at the kitchen sink, she indicated. As for bathing, he didn't know what she did—or what he would do. He saw no sign of a bath or shower.

His assigned bedroom was cramped. It apparently belonged to her son. Ken couldn't make out where the son was but gathered that he stayed there regularly. The bed was lumpy in places, and short. His six-foot-one frame required him to curl up more than he usually would. But it was clean. She provided him with two blankets she got from somewhere in the small house. There were no sheets.

☙☙

His sleepy recollection reminded him that while he knew where he was, he had not a clue where his nine students and fellow chaperone might be. Still, there was nothing to be done about that now. Something else asserted itself through his sleepiness; he needed the outhouse.

Making sure he was decently attired, he opened the bedroom door, which led into the small dining area.

Ana turned from the small gas stove, greeting him brightly: "*A, buenas dias!*"

"*Buenas dias,*" he responded. At least he knew to say that much.

She then gestured toward the stove, rubbed her stomach briefly, and asked, "*Hambre?*"

"Yes, er . . . *si,*" he said. But realizing his bathroom need was growing in urgency, he pointed to the kitchen door. She understood and let him squeeze past.

Later, after a breakfast of tortillas, with beans, rice and what he thought was a version of an omelet, Ken tried to help with dishes, but with unmistakable authority Ana waved him off. As she cleared the table, something outside caught her eye and she became noticeably animated. She put down the last of the dishes and opened the front door. Approaching the house was a white man, in his fifties or maybe early sixties, with a full head of white hair.

When he got to the door he and Ana greeted each other enthusiastically. He bent slightly so they could give each other an "air cheek kiss"— touching their cheeks and kissing the air. They took each other's hands. Ana waved to Ken and said, "*El es Juan, mi amigo.*"

"Juan" followed Ana into the house and stepped energetically toward Ken. He held out his hand and said in a flat Midwestern accent, "John, John Braxton, at your service, sir."

"Wow, am I glad to hear an English-speaker," Ken said. "Ken Barker," he said, putting out his hand.

"I gather you and your group have had a bit of a misadventure," the newcomer said. "Got lost or something. They brought me in as your UN translator. Ana," he said, nodding in her direction, "came to me just after 5:30 to tell me what she could of your story.

"Oh, don't look surprised; we all get up early here. She told me to show up round about 8. So here I am." Braxton paused. "So then, you're lost?" His question was asked with a tone of concern, not critique.

Ken told him his, and the group's, story. When he got to the part about arriving at San Gabriel, Braxton raised his hand to interrupt: "Let me see your air ticket, will you. Or e-ticket or whatever they give you these days."

Ken went to the bedroom, dug around for a moment or two in the section of his bag containing his documents and found his boarding passes from yesterday and the schedule from the travel agent. He took them to the dining room, where Braxton sat drinking a cup of coffee freshly poured in Ken's brief absence. Without his asking, Ana handed Ken a cup too.

Braxton took the paperwork and after just a moment said, "Yes, I see; exactly what I suspected. You didn't make any mistakes. You came to Santa Gabriella just as your ticket indicates. Trouble is, you should have flown into San Gabriel—and that's about 300 kilometers in the other direction, across the mountains. Your travel agent sent you to the wrong airport."

"But what about San Pedro?" Ken asked.

"Well, no mystery there," Braxton replied. "When you realize this country must have—who knows—maybe three, four dozen 'San Pedros,' from the tiniest of villages to a couple of pretty sizable towns, it's no surprise that your taxi drivers found one within driving distance."

Braxton added, "It's a fairly common mistake, people mixing up San Gabriel and Santa Gabriella. Stupid move, having two airports in one country with virtually identical names. Some state senator insisted on Santa Gabriella getting its own international airport, the one you flew into, and got huge kickbacks behind the scenes when the airport was built. Nasty stuff, but typical."

Braxton chuckled to himself: "The airport code for Santa Gabriella is GVV. The story is someone in the country's aviation authority assigned the airport those letters, pretending they didn't know it's an abbreviation for a common Spanish three-word obscene phrase. So the corrupt senator is remembered in a way he didn't expect. But that's another story."

Braxton continued, "It's one thing to mix up Pueblo in Colorado, with Puebla in Mexico. But any travel agent would know the difference—that if you're in the States you'd need a passport to get to one but not to the other. Understandable mistake your agent made, when you think about it."

If Braxton's explanation helped Ken suddenly see the light, the bemused youth pastor didn't for one moment like what the light illuminated. His mind was processing a whirl of "what now?" questions. But first he found the need to confirm the reality of his plight.

"So we've come to help the wrong village?" he said, stating the obvious just to clarify the magnitude of his (and, of course, the group's) situation.

Braxton nodded.

"And all the supplies and money for accommodation and meals and everything are sitting at another San Pedro, hundreds of miles, um, kilometers from here?"

Again, Braxton nodded.

Ken was only beginning to grasp the extent of the blunder. He remembered reading once something about problems: "A problem is something you could do something about; everything else is a fact of life." He was not for an instant willing to accept as a fact of life that they were stuck in the wrong San Pedro and that all the planning and expense of this trip was now wasted. And that he would have to explain to the folks back home in a week's time that this was the mission trip that wasn't. Does one sue the kindly Christian travel agent whose fault this was? That question would wait. What wouldn't, he realized, is what to do *now* about addressing this problem.

Another, more immediate, problem, was his coffee. It was strangely bitter and gritty and cloyingly sweet at the same time. He now recalled he had seen Ana putting about four spoonfuls of sugar into his cup before handing it to him. He was going to have to deal with local tastes in coffee sip by sip.

Ken directed his attention back to Braxton: "I suppose the first thing is to phone our contact in the other San Pedro   ." His voice trailed off as he realized for the first time that the assumptions he'd made about Ricardo's incompetence were not only totally unjustified; Ricardo himself would have no doubt have been hitting the phones himself last night, presumably trying to call the people at Mission Matchers and Pastor Lawrence—whose number he'd given Ricardo as an emergency contact. Ken could only guess at the level of consternation that those phone calls must have generated.

"Yes, I need to phone various people, and right away . . . And we need to find a way to get to the other San Pedro."

Braxton laughed. "You'd be better off using smoke signals or jungle drums, young fellow. Our San Pedro is in a dip. There's no signal here. And hardly anyone here has a cellphone. No point, when you think of it." He added, "Oh some folks do, but only for when they go into Santa Gabriella. And of course there'd be pay phones in Santa Gabriella that you could normally use . . ." The way he said those last words was troublingly tentative.

"What do you mean '*normally* use'?" Ken asked.

"Ah, yes," said Braxton. "You may have noticed a little damp weather last night." Ken wasn't sure how much he appreciated Braxton's wry sense of humor, especially given the gravity of his situation. "Well, it's the rainy season here, unlike the other side of the mountains. And it's been raining solidly for a week. By now the bridge down by San Miguel will be flooded, that's for sure.

"To be honest, I'm amazed your taxis could get you here last night. The drivers obviously didn't know about the San Miguel bridge. It's far enough out of their normal range, so I wouldn't expect them to know. Otherwise they would never have considered bringing you here. For all I know, the river may have flooded before they could make it back last night."

Ken was fast approaching a state of total disbelief: "You mean there's no way I can phone people to tell them where we are? And that we're stuck here for who knows how long?"

Braxton responded, "Well, you're right about the phone. And how long are you stuck? Maybe two, three days. Hard to tell. Sometimes the bridge clears pretty quickly."

Ken asked with heightened exasperation: "And there's *no* other way to reach the outside world?"

"Afraid not," came Braxton's laconic but not unsympathetic reply.

"How can these people survive being cut off from the rest of the world?" Ken said, expressing a disbelieving frustration more than a question.

But Braxton took it as a question and said, "That's how humankind has existed for thousands upon thousands of years. These people are quite used to it. In fact, they're amused by the obsession of those who demand to be connected twenty-four hours a day. They even feel sorry for people like you."

He continued, "I mean, Ana and everyone else in the village is getting on with life. They're perfectly self-contained here. They're not worried about the bridge being out. To them, that's just one of those things."

A question reasserted itself in Ken's mind: He had wondered earlier who this fellow was and what he was doing in this obscure, out-of-the way village. But as Braxton made clear for Ken the suddenly changed nature of the mission trip, he set aside for the moment his curiosity about Braxton. Given the realities he now faced, there was ample time to hear this man's story later.

8

The Braxton Diatribe

Sunday Morning

KEN REMEMBERED THAT THE group's plan was to lead the service this morning at the other San Pedro church. Now, accepting that was impossible, he confirmed with Braxton what he thought Ana told him last night: "And church this morning is at 11, right?"

"Well, in principle, anyway. More likely 11:20, 11:30," Braxton replied. "Just takes a while to get going. After all, nobody's in a hurry."

"That's when I can get the group together, explain the situation, and look at our options—whatever they are . . ." Ken said. Then he added, "What *are* our options?"

"You're here until Tuesday, maybe Wednesday—until the bridge clears. You may have noticed: Not a single car or truck has driven by this morning, either way," Braxton said. "The locals know it's pointless to head to the town and the people in town couldn't get through even if they wanted to."

Depending on when the bridge cleared, it would within two or three days be possible for Ken to find a ride into town, make his phone calls and see if he still could arrange to take the group to the other San Pedro—for what might be another two or three days at the most. And maybe he could re-connect the group with their luggage.

Ana interrupted to pour more coffee in Ken's and Braxton's mugs. Ken fortunately caught her in time, to gesture he'd forego a refill, thank you very much.

"And here, what could we do here?" he asked Braxton. "We've come to help."

Braxton laughed. "Seems like you're the ones needing all the help. You've arrived in the wrong place, you don't speak the language, you don't know the culture. For example, you probably don't know that Ana took a great risk having you spend last night here. The word is already all around the village about the group of gringos."

Braxton paused for breath. "And the fact that an adult male who's not family stayed in her house puts her reputation on the line. Same for any of the other women who may have taken those boys into their homes. Just not done. If those inclined to gossip want to have fun with this, Ana could have a tough time with snide remarks, rumors, and so on. But she didn't hesitate to take that risk. She's that kind of woman. She saw your need and reached out to you in Christian grace. Bet you didn't see any risk in what she was doing, did you?"

Ken was squirming. He reluctantly nodded his agreement.

Whether Braxton sensed Ken's discomfort or not, he wasn't letting up: "And even if you were in the right place, my guess is that you'd know nobody. Am I right?"

Ken answered, "Well, we have a contact person, and we've spoken with him several times."

Braxton said, "No, what I mean is any kind of relationship. Nobody in your group or church has been there before, yes?"

Ken began, "Well . . ." when Braxton interrupted: "And I suppose you went through one of those organizations that plays matchmaker, for a fee, of course—putting wealthy, well-intending Americans in touch with complete strangers in desperately poor communities that are willing to take any help and support they can get."

Ken's indignation rose yet higher: "Aren't you being terribly cynical?"

Braxton responded: "Am I? What have I said that's untrue? Oh, one other thing: You'd be bringing help for your painting project that simply isn't needed. You think the people in the other San Pedro don't know how to paint?"

He looked to Ken for affirmation of his point. Getting none, he added, "One thing this country has is an abundance of unskilled labor. Painting's easy stuff. Now, taking a dental clinic or a couple of pediatricians to a village—that's different. Got any dentists or hygienists or pediatric nurses in your group? No, didn't think so.

"But you and your missionaries think you can parachute in here and, as you put it, 'help'?"

Braxton paused. Before he could re-load, Ken said, "Well, we were going to lead the church service and do a Vacation Bible School with the kids."

"Yes, I forgot about the mandatory VBS. Every group has to do one of those, right? And I bet you brought an entire menagerie of puppets, now lying in luggage claim at the airport. Yes?"

Ken's awkwardness rose to new levels. How much of Braxton's statements were an accurate assessment of reality and how much was a product of his own, obviously anti-missionary bias and hostility? He couldn't tell.

But Braxton wasn't done. "And your question, 'What could you do here'?" he said. "I don't know. You'd need to speak to the church leaders about that. Maybe after church. They don't have a minister. But Alfredo Morales serves as a kind of pastor. He's clearly their leader. They'll have ideas."

Fortunately for Ken, Braxton seemed to be done with his diatribe. He feared that Braxton might resume it later. Half of him wanted to know who this fellow was, and his story, and the source of his hostility. But the other half was afraid to encounter another of Braxton's fusillades; he didn't know what more ammunition he might have after reloading.

The silence between them was strained. Ana picked up on the tension and offered yet more coffee. Against his better judgment, Ken accepted half a cup before signaling to Ana to stop pouring.

"Look," Braxton said. "Believe it or not, I admire what you're doing. Even though I don't like your way of doing it, it's still far better than other people's ways of *not* doing it—those people who could take the risks and put up with the discomfort and dislocation that you're willing to face but choose to stay at home watching Netflix. So, yes, I'm impressed. But we'll talk more later." That clearly marked the end of that conversation or, more correctly, a broadside. Ken felt a palpable sense of relief but Braxton's criticisms had cut deeply; they were all exactly on target, both for the group and for him as its leader. Though he hated to admit it, he was embarrassed at the model of missions he had bought into and was now obliged to implement.

Braxton then spoke at some length with Ana before turning back to Ken. "I'll be off now. Ana will get you to church round about 11. The rest of your group should be there and either before or after the service you can talk with Alfredo and the women. Between you and me," he said, lowering his voice, "the women run the church anyway."

He shook Ken's hand, gave a departing air-kiss to Ana, and left.

9

—

Ricardo's Troubled Morning

Sunday Morning

RICARDO WOKE EARLY. DESPITE the assurances he had given Pastor Lawrence, he was concerned. As soon as he thought the airport would have come back to life, he began phoning: first, the Delta office, then a more general airport number. Nobody could shed any light on the First Church group. No flights from the United States were due all of today; Sunday was a quiet air traffic day, the Delta official said.

Ricardo's next move was to contact his boss at Mission Matchers, in Houston, Clara Small. She was sympathetic to Ricardo's plight and said she'd make some enquiries about the group's connections. She had a contact at Delta who could track the group's actual, as opposed to booked, itinerary. "I just hope he's available today," she said. "It may be that I can reach him only tomorrow and I may struggle to get anything from an official who's ultra-careful about giving out customer info. But I'll try and get back to you."

With Clara working the US angle, and Ricardo pursuing things in San Gabriel, they were doing all they could.

10

———

Updating the Parents

Sunday Morning

DURING ANNOUNCEMENT TIME AT church on Sunday morning, Pastor Lawrence—in as matter-of-fact a tone as he could muster—asked all the parents of the mission group to remain after church for a brief word. Even though he sounded as under-stated as he hoped, he left at least some of the more anxious parents, especially Eileen Sanker, Kristen's Mom, speculating on what could be wrong. She couldn't focus on anything in Pastor Lawrence's sermon, which was a pity as today he had excelled himself with a thoughtful and provocative message on faith in times of uncertainty.

After the service they squeezed into the pastor's study, where he began by assuring them that he had no reason for concern but wanted to update them on his messages from Ricardo: The group had not arrived. By itself, that needn't have caused alarm. Often things went awry in air travel. But what rattled the group, and especially Eileen Sanker, was when he felt compelled to tell them Part B: Nobody knew where they were.

On hearing this, Eileen Sanker gave a gasp and for the second consecutive day began crying in front of her fellow church members. Fortunately, Kyra's four-year-old brother Gary wasn't in attendance to compound Mrs. Sanker's plight.

The others began peppering the pastor with questions.

"How could they not have arrived?"

"Haven't we heard from Ken? Why hasn't he phoned us if there's a problem?"

"What about this Ricardo fellow; what's he doing to find them?"

Joachim Estes, Zach's dad, surreptitiously scanned his smart phone for any stories about plane crashes and, finding none, thought it best to not even raise this possibility to the other parents.

The questions kept coming.

"Well, pastor, what do *you* plan to do about this?"

"And what exactly is this Mission Matchers organization anyway? What do we know about them?"

Estes, ex-military and now a real estate broker, was known to everyone as a man of calm action. He was quietly glad he'd made Zach take out travel insurance for this trip, the only team member to do so. Again, he was tactful enough not to mention this.

But he now felt compelled to speak up.

"Listen everyone, there's no good speculating on what might have happened. Let's stick to what we know—and all we know is that the group hasn't arrived. There's nothing any of us can do right now until we learn more." Taking charge of the conversation and the collective mood, he continued: "I, for one, am sure there's a reasonable explanation. Remember, they're in a developing country; communications aren't always what we're used to. There are language differences. They're in sensible hands with Ken as their leader; I know I wouldn't have let Zach go on this trip if I weren't confident in Ken's leadership.

"So let's just be patient and calm. Pastor Lawrence knows of our concern and it goes without saying that he'll let all of us know as soon as he gets any updates."

Several in the group nodded their agreement and a willingness to accept the status quo of their present ignorance. One exception was Eileen Sanker, whose muffled sobs continued until the group began dispersing a few minutes later—following Pastor Lawrence's prayer for the group's wellbeing and for God's peace for each of the parents as they waited.

As they were leaving Andre Borgvik, Heidi's father, spoke up. He was something of a hot-head, an impulsive and forceful man, who had asked some of the most hostile questions.

"Praying is all good and well, but I can't believe what's happening, Pastor. You're saying you have no idea where our children are. You can't tell us if Heidi and the other kids are safe. Are they lost? Or heaven forbid, kidnapped, or even worse, dead?"

Eileen Sanker emitted a combination gasp and sob.

Pastor Lawrence tried to sooth Andre but without success.

Andre continued: "This just isn't acceptable, you know. Who are these people who're supposed to be looking after our kids? What do you know about them—I mean, *really* know about them?"

Before the Pastor could respond, Andre answered his own question: "Nothing, right? We've entrusted our kids to a bunch of strangers, in a foreign, Third World country."

He paused; the rest of the parents, who except for Eileen Sanker, had taken the pastor's news calmly, now began to contemplate the kind of worst-case scenarios that Andre mentioned.

"Look," said Pastor Lawrence, with his own equanimity now verging into testiness, "as I said, there's nothing else we can tell you. As soon as we learn anything . . ."

Andre cut him short: "This just isn't good enough. I want to know, *where is my daughter*?" Murmurs and affirmative mutterings followed.

Joachim Estes cut them short. "It's OK, everyone. Let's just calm down. Pastor has assured us that he'll tell us of what's happening as soon as he learns what's going on." His unruffled, authoritative manner checked the rising discontent and potential parental mutiny.

He continued: "And as I said earlier, the group is in good hands with Ken. They'll be fine. We are people of faith, remember; let's show a little more faith that God knows their situation and that they're in his hands."

Nobody dared contradict his theology and Pastor Lawrence repeated his assurance that he'd let the group know as soon as he heard from Ken or the Mission Matchers people. More grateful to Estes than he'd care to say openly, he dismissed the group, before heading home and unloading on his wife, Crystal, about Andre Borgvik.

"Every church, I guess, has its thorn in the flesh." Then, lapsing into a rare moment of crudity, he added: "But Borgvik's not just a thorn, he's a first-rate prick."

Crystal said, "Yes, dear," and continued preparing lunch.

11

Church at 11, Sort Of

Sunday Morning

KEN TOOK SOME TIME to sort through his carry-on bag and realized he had only one change of clothing. He thought he'd brought more, following the recommended packing list that he had written. Laundry needs would soon loom large.

He looked over his trip binder in his bedroom. It would have been more comfortable sitting at the small dining room table but he didn't want to get in Ana's way as she busied herself with various chores. He perused the detailed plans he, Irma and Ricardo had worked out, wondering what bits of the week might yet be salvaged. Assuming Braxton was right, getting to the other San Pedro might be out of the question. Even if they could get to the airport in time, the trip budget almost certainly couldn't stand a round-trip ticket for eleven of them to the other San Pedro—this was assuming they needed to fly home from Santa Gabriella. So, the group's main goal, painting the church, was out. Could they still do the VBS? Maybe. Perhaps Alfredo and the women would have some ideas. After all, the First Church group *had* come to help.

☙❧

Able to talk about little, Ken and Ana minimized attempts at conversation for the couple of hours that remained until 11. Repeatedly, they exchanged the smiles that serve as the primary social lubricant between language-barriered individuals, with each in effect saying, "You know, I'd love talking with you;

I think you and I have much we could share. Such a shame, this Tower of Babel curse, not so?" And a smile is returned, echoing that sentiment.

Ken spent a while in his room, sitting on his bed, doing his regular Bible reading despite his sense of spiritual discombobulation. The Bible reading guide he was following steered him toward an obscure passage in Ezekiel, which despite his every effort yielded no insight or application to his and the group's plight. In prayer too he found no insights or any particular direction, except for a sense that he should merely wait for God to reveal the next steps. For despite his confusion, he was assured that God had at the very least permitted this disaster to unfold, if not actually willed it.

His thoughts drifted back to his seminary training. Was there anything from those hours spent studying Old and New Testament, exegesis and hermeneutics, homiletics, pastoral theology or even Greek and Hebrew that could help him now? Nothing. If only there were a course he could have taken, listed in the seminary catalog as, "Things That Can Go Wrong on Mission Trips—501; three credits, offered fall in even years." Maybe by the end of this week he'd even be qualified to teach it.

He thought of his favorite professor, old Smitty, and how he might handle the current fiasco. If they had taken "most popular professor" votes at the seminary, Smitty would have been a perennial winner. His real-world experience of eighteen years in the pastorate merged with his scholarly credentials to yield what a student once called "a perfectly tuned wisdom machine." More formally known as Professor Augustus Randolph Smith, he never attained the heights of academe for which he was naturally predisposed. Instead, he chose to do minimal publishing and focused on honing his already superb, intuitive skills as a teacher. Even Ken's more academically inclined classmates looked at Smitty as a model for the kind of Christian they'd want to be as they grew into their ministries.

Students' notes were packed with his aphorisms, insights and words of counsel. One of his favorite sayings was, "If you think God's too small for your problem, it's time for a new God." Another was, "And you think this took God *by surprise*?"—which he'd always ask with his thin eyebrows raised what seemed like a full two inches into his forehead.

Ken smiled at this recollection. He thought of another of Smitty's sayings about approaching pastoral problems: "Get your ego out, get God in." That certainly applied right now, he confessed. Reluctantly, he conceded that he was as much concerned with what the group, the parents, and especially Pastor Lawrence would think about his leadership. His first mission trip was likely to be his last at First Church. This year could also be his last. He could easily imagine Heidi's dad, Andre Borgvik sitting in Pastor Lawrence's office, banging his fist on the pastor's desk and demanding Ken's head on a platter—something for which there was an excellent biblical precedent, he would no doubt remind Pastor Lawrence. And he thought of the alarm circulating among the nine church families whose responses would undoubtedly include a mix of panic, terror, anger and a range of other perfectly understandable reactions. Their frustration, following calls either from Ricardo or Mission Matchers, or both, would lead to wild speculations. Ken could picture Annabel's mom wanting to contact the US State Department, their local Congressman, and if necessary the White House itself.

Ana interrupted Ken's unhappy reverie with a gesture indicating that it was time to go. Ken checked his watch; to his surprise, it said 11:17. But Ana wasn't in the least rushed, so he made a quick visit to the outhouse, not knowing what facilities the church might have, and joined Ana on a silent three-minute walk to church. Despite the heavy rain from the previous night, and who knows how many days and nights before that, the ground was still relatively dry and hard in places, although there was also much mud. It was difficult to believe that the critical bridge of which Braxton had spoken was impassable; yet Ken had no reason to doubt the older man's word. He fully accepted that the group was stuck in San Pedro. But he wasn't willing to accept that they were doomed to a season of pathetic inactivity, totally dependent on the mercy and grace of these strangers. He was therefore all the more eager to meet Alfredo and learn how he could help the group.

⚭

For the first time Ken saw San Pedro in daylight. It was much as he expected, with a predominance of concrete block houses, like Ana's. Interspersed among them were a few adobe homes, some of which were painted in bright colors. Most of the houses, however, were the dull grey of concrete. Two other buildings he noticed were within easy walking distance from the house. One was the church where the taxis had dropped them last night, and their immediate destination. The other was the small multi-purpose building that served as the community's pub, restaurant and store—and social hub. That's where Carlos the driver had asked for directions some fourteen hours earlier.

The street on which they trudged toward the church was San Pedro's main thoroughfare. If he'd looked behind him, he would have noticed the village's two other non-residential buildings: the elementary school, which served not only this village but several others nearby, and the San Felipe Catholic church.

Taking in his surroundings he assumed this village, the "wrong" San Pedro, probably looked much like the "correct" one. Then he acknowledged those were *his* terms; and this village's 400 other residents wouldn't have seen their community that way; this was *home*, not somewhere "wrong." If anything was awry about the situation, it was the intrusion of Ken's cadre of eleven Americans who had shown up uninvited and unexpected. Now, facing this reality, Ken's primary task was to ameliorate this wrong that he had perpetrated.

When Ken and arrived at the church, five other members of the group had already assembled. They were clustered outside the church, standing to the left of the entrance. At least they were alive and had made it through their first night, Ken thought. Six more nights to go. They were eagerly exchanging their tales of survival in a strange land.

Without exception they spoke of the kindness their hosts showed them. Language difficulties were an issue for each of the kids, less so for Sissy, whose college level Spanish was largely moribund. Two of the girls, Sharon and Kristen, told how they shared a bed while their host mom slept on a couch—despite the girls' protestations. Some registered awkwardness at the absence of indoor bathrooms and the need to visit an outhouse, which was the norm in San Pedro, and in most small villages throughout the country.

Tim, who was a vegetarian, described how he was served some un-identifiable meat dish for breakfast, which he thought consisted of ground beef, and had forced himself to eat it out of politeness. Most of the group, though, said they had been fed some combination of rice, beans, eggs and tortillas. As Sharon put it, "I really appreciated getting food I could understand."

Ken greeted each of them warmly, assuring himself of their wellbeing, and all the while looking out for someone who resembled a pastor.

Zach spoke for the students when he asked, "So, what's happening, what's going on?"

Ken took a couple of minutes to recount briefly what John Braxton had told him, as clearly and dispassionately as he could. That is, the organizational implications of their plight; he didn't report on Braxton's philosophy of missions.

"You mean we're in the wrong village?" Kyra asked in a voice that mixed alarm, astonishment and disbelief in equal proportions, confirming what was apparent the previous night and what Ken had just announced.

"Yes," said Ken, repeating the explanation of the airport mix-up, and adding that he didn't know what their next steps were. "I hope to learn more from the pastor, as soon as I can chat with him."

Zach asked, "Are we going to spend our week doing our mission stuff here?"

Ken responded, drawing on what he knew would need to be a deep well of patience: "Well, as I said, I just don't know. I need to talk with the pastor. Haven't had the chance to do that yet."

Predictably enough, Heidi asked, "And what about the puppets?" Tempted to say something like "That's the least of my concerns right now," Ken managed a more gracious response: "Well, they'll still be at the airport." Seeing Heidi's visible distress, even though she had been aware since last night that the puppets probably hadn't yet made it to the Santa Gabriella airport, he added, "Well, like us they at least have each other." He immediately regretted his flip remark. But to his surprise Heidi found this comforting.

Aware that he was in danger of lapsing into even more overt snippiness or sarcasm, he decided he had better leave the group and seek out the pastor to whom he kept referring but still hadn't met.

Even though it was now approaching 11:30, nobody was in any rush to get going with the service, least of all Pastor Alfredo—whom Ken now identified inside. As Ken entered the church he saw that it was different from last night. A couple of colorful banners, whose symbolism wasn't immediately clear to Ken, hung from hooks on the building's relatively low ceiling. Someone was playing soft, worshipful music on a keyboard, which Ken didn't think was there the previous night. And a table at the back had urns for coffee, hot water and packets of tea and sweetener. Unlike the emptiness the church conveyed last night, when only the five women were at their meeting, about forty people now occupied the space. They huddled in conversations of two or three, finding their own spaces as would individuals in an elevator. The church hummed with conversation, interspersed with frequent laughter.

Ken scanned the sanctuary for Ana. He saw her standing at the front of the church, where a nondescript man in his forties, perhaps, stood speaking earnestly with her and another woman whom Ken recognized as another of the host moms, as he now thought of them. The man, whom Ken rightly assumed was Alfredo, noticed Ken and immediately lit up and waved a welcoming hand. He excused himself from the two women and strode briskly toward Ken, shaking him warmly with one hand and firmly grasping Ken's shoulder with the other.

"Welcome, welcome," he said. "Welcome in San Pedro, even if it is a mistake," he added, smiling. Ken was grateful for his English fluency.

Alfredo added, "We must talk much—after church, yes?" It was an announcement more than a question.

"Yes, *si*," said Ken.

"But first we have church, yes?"

"Yes," said Ken.

More people were trickling in and Ken noticed that even from outside the students had sensed the service was about to start, judging from the increased flow of people into the sanctuary.

By now the congregation was getting settled. For the first time, Ken realized that men and older boys were drifting to the chairs on the left, as you faced the front; women, girls, and younger children were on the right. Ana pointed to the left, making sure Ken understood the seating arrangements. He noted both that the rest of the group had now arrived, including Sissy, and that they had all figured out where to sit.

"So," Ken thought, "service first, explanations later."

1 2

———

Worship and a Village History Lesson

Sunday Morning

KEN WAS MOSTLY RIGHT: Even before the worship service came Pastor Alfredo's welcome. It was enthusiastic, as he gestured to Ken and the group, with a sweep of his arms, accompanied by an animated barrage of Spanish totally lost on Ken. He thought he heard Alfredo mention his name but that was muffled by the tail-end of one of several bouts of good-natured laughter from the congregation—jokes whose tone seemed kindly, not cruel. Then Alfredo paused and, stretching his right hand toward Ken, he said in English what he had just said in Spanish: "Welcome, friends, brothers and sisters in Christ." Applause followed and Ken stood to acknowledge this greeting; the group followed his cue and stood, hesitantly at first, as unsure about how to respond to this situation as they were about everything else in this new and unfamiliar world.

Then the service itself began. Although entirely in Spanish, its format was recognizable enough: an opening prayer, a Bible reading, twenty to twenty-five minutes of worship songs (the melodies of at least two of which Ken recognized), and an offering. Ken was grateful to have some local currency, thanks to Ricardo's advice, and he made what he hoped was an appropriate contribution on behalf of the group.

Everyone stood during the music, except for a few moms nursing babes or holding wriggly toddlers, and a few elderly folk. Then, quite unexpectedly, the pastor said something and the congregation acted as if they had been dismissed. Taken aback, Ken wondered, "No sermon?"

43

The congregation drifted toward the back of the church to the coffee table, which had mysteriously acquired several plates of pastries since Ken had last looked.

"What's going on?" said Bill, who was sitting next to Ken.

"I'm guessing it's a coffee break," Ken replied. He was right. He, the students and Sissy made their way along with everyone else to the table, encouraged by the smiles and hand gestures of many in the congregation. Plied with coffee or tea, and a hard-to-define pastry with caraway seeds, they huddled together on their own. The language barrier was palpable. One elderly man approached the students and, shaking their hands in welcome, began a halting conversation in English. It was obvious that nobody else felt able even to try conversing with the group, although the students sensed that despite their status as strangers, people felt warmly toward them.

Twenty minutes later the pastor summoned the congregation back to their seats and then began another scripture reading (from Matthew's gospel, as best Ken could tell) and a sermon. The congregation was clearly engaged in the message, which the visitors thought sounded articulate and forceful—and long; Ken timed it, surreptitiously, at thirty-seven minutes. A final song and they were done. (Ken later learned Alfredo had shortened the sermon considerably out of deference to the guests.)

The congregation milled around, chatting with each other. More people came up to the students to welcome them with smiles and short Spanish greetings that the group could acknowledge only with reciprocated smiles. The pastor remained at the front of the church, gathering papers and chatting briefly to the man at the keyboard.

Ken decided to give Alfredo some space and moved outside, following the group. He'd heard some quiet voices and some subdued hustle and bustle during the service but paid no attention to what he assumed was routine activity. But he was astonished to see the transformation. Set up on the concrete patio were three tables, filled with food. Off to the side, still on the patio and avoiding the ground muddied by last night's rain, was a table of Styrofoam cups and bottles of soft drinks. He identified some Coke but couldn't tell what the others were. Some women he didn't recognize were putting final touches to the meal; one was putting paper plates and plastic knives and forks at another small table. Standing back near the road were small clusters of men, chatting quietly out of respect for the service that had now ended.

Ken couldn't be sure but he thought both the men and women were more formally dressed than those in Alfredo's congregation. But of one thing he was certain: They were all about to be attendees at a feast. Fleetingly, he thought it might be in the group's honor. But then he realized their arrival only last night would have made it impossible for their hosts to organize this impromptu fiesta. (At least he knew that word of Spanish.) And who was this other group?

Seeing Alfredo emerge from the church, Ken approached him. The pastor was now ready to engage so Ken pointed to the food and the women attending to the final preparations, and asked, "*Que es?*" For now, his curiosity trumped even his organizational dilemma and his question was an easy conversation starter.

Alfredo laughed and said, "*Si, es una fiesta.*" This much Ken already knew, wishing he could translate "And would you please take the next step and explain the occasion of these festivities?" But Alfredo waved to a portly man who had just entered the church grounds. If Ken was uncertain about the dress standards for this group who had joined Alfredo's congregation, there was no mistaking this newcomer's attire. He was a priest, still wearing his clerical collar and what had once been a high-quality, beautifully embroidered cassock but now showing the beginnings of shabbiness. On his head was a four-pointed black hat, which Ken later learned was called a biretta.

As the man strode towards them, Alfredo said by way of explanation as much as introduction, "*Padre Gonzalez—Catolico.*"

Fr. Gonzalez, Ken could tell instantly, was someone of substance, beginning with a firm but not brutal handshake, and a quite extraordinary warmth. His eyes simultaneously welcomed and assessed you, Ken thought, as the handshake continued longer than Ken expected.

"Ken, er . . . Kendall Barker," he said, feeling a need to display at least some formality in the priest's presence.

"Yes, Mr. Barker—the shepherd of the lost sheep," Gonzalez said, not unkindly but with humor that Ken understood and acknowledged.

Even this single sentence told Ken that the priest's English was not only excellent but also curiously unaccented.

"You're in bit of a pickle, I understand," Gonzalez added, now impressing Ken with his use of idiom.

"Yes," Ken said. "It's quite a story. We flew into the wrong airport."

"The wrong airport?"

"Well, we flew to the airport we thought we were going to, but it turns out we shouldn't have been going to," Ken said. Seeing Gonzalez's puzzlement, he added: "What happened is that our travel agent booked us into Santa Gabriella but it should have been San Gabriel, the other side of the mountains."

"I see," the priest said. "Yes, I've heard of that happening before. Not often, and only with people from outside the country." He sounded sympathetic, not judgmental. "But the question is what are we going to do with you now? Pastor Alfredo told me a bit about your plight. You're on a church mission trip, I think he said. Yes?"

"Yes," Ken said, immensely grateful to be talking with another fluent English speaker. Although he was saying nothing, Alfredo appeared to be tracking well enough. Now and again Gonzalez would briefly explain something to the pastor in Spanish but for the most part Alfredo nodded repeatedly to signify he was getting the gist of things.

Gonzalez continued: "I know some of the families in Pastor Alfredo's church helped out with accommodation last night, in an emergency. But they can't all do that for however long you will be here, which will be at least a few days. So about half of you will come and stay with some of our families."

"We worked it out before our services this morning." It turned out that the Catholic service had finished about an hour earlier, which gave Gonzalez's parishioners time to set up the food.

Ken's reaction was an unprecedented mix of deep gratitude at yet more grace being extended to his group, with an uncertainty about how the folks back home would respond to half the group staying with Catholic families.

Sensing what must have been a glimmer of hesitation on Ken's face, the priest added, "Not to worry; Pastor Alfredo and I have got it all worked out." Then he added, articulating Ken's unspoken awkwardness far more perceptively than he would like to admit, "And I think you'll find that the gap between evangelicals and Catholics in our village is far smaller than you might expect."

Ken still had no explanation for the fiesta, which clearly was about to begin. One of the Catholic women approached her priest and said, "*Estamos listos, padre.*"

Gonzalez turned to Ken and said, "She tells me they're ready. So I need to give the blessing. I'll be right back."

He got everyone's attention and, adopting a more formal pose and manner, raised his hands and said, "*Oremos.*" Heads bowed, and Gonzalez gave a brief prayer, which included in English a word of thanks to God for bringing the visitors into their midst—which he then repeated in Spanish.

He turned his attention again to Ken and said, "And I imagine you're wanting to know what's happening here today?"

Ken nodded.

"What we're doing has a long history but I'll keep it short. But come, let's get our food."

They joined the line, along with Ken's group, whom the locals invited to the front of the line.

Ken, Alfredo and Gonzalez picked up plates, napkins, knives and forks and proceeded to load their plates. While they were still doing so the priest resumed the conversation.

"During the civil war our village was mostly on the fringes of the brutality. But not always. Sometimes the guerillas would hide here and the paramilitary would seek those they thought were sheltering them. And you know the story: If they thought you were guilty, they'd take you out, line up the entire village, and shoot you as an example.

"Sometimes people from other villages who were fleeing the paramilitary would come here and seek sanctuary, and both the evangelicals and the Catholics in town didn't hesitate to help—knowing they could be killed. And sometimes they were."

By now, Gonzalez had steered Ken toward a bench. They and Alfredo sat and the priest resumed his account. "We're a small village, only 400 people or so, including children. We were quite a bit smaller back then. But fourteen of our men were murdered. And they didn't just kill the men, they'd make their wives and children watch. Or if they were younger they'd make their parents and brothers and sisters watch. Three or four of those killed were teenagers."

Ken saw an incongruity between the horror of the priest's story and the celebratory atmosphere all around him. Members from the two congregations were mingling, catching up with each other over this shared meal, just like any potluck at any church back home, he thought.

"We got through that time of horror in our village. But only with the understanding that when someone was fleeing from the paramilitary, you would take care of him as best you could. It didn't matter if he was Catholic or Protestant."

Realizing he was ignoring his meal, the priest took another bite.

"Where was I? Oh yes, it was those awful days that pulled us together. We developed enormous respect for the courage that each side showed, and the risks they took—which as I said led to fourteen of our people being killed."

He continued: "So what has that got to do with today's fiesta? When the war ended, my predecessor and a previous leader of the evangelicals met and said that once a month we must have a fiesta to celebrate the good things we did together, and for each other, and to honor the lives of those who were executed. So we do that each month, except for December. Also, we skip a month for Easter. We take turns and this month it's our turn to bring the food.

"Not all villages were like that, though," he added. "Actually, ours was very much the exception. And I can say that confidently because I wasn't here and can't take any credit for the courage they showed."

Ken suddenly realized he'd made no progress with the two church leaders regarding the mission group's plight and the group's next steps. Captivated though he was by the priest's account of village history, he'd almost forgotten the very reason he and his group were in San Pedro—even if it were the *wrong* San Pedro.

So after what he hoped was a respectful silence, he got Gonzalez's and Alfredo's joint attention and asked, "So tell me, do you have any ideas about what our group can do?" They conferred briefly, nodded in agreement, and turned to Ken.

Once again, it was Gonzalez who spoke: "Today is Sunday. It's the Sabbath. We won't do any work today. How about we talk about this tomorrow? Monday is a day to work, *si*?"

Ken couldn't disagree with the logic but it still gave him no answers—or even the hint of an answer on how they could spend their time meaningfully. He still had nothing to tell the group, whom he could see huddled about twenty yards away. One of the more forceful Catholic women kept reappearing to gesture to the group to get more food. But other than this interaction, Ken's mini-flock sat to the side, while the men, women and children from the two congregations engaged in conversations, including some spirited but apparently good-natured arguments, while they watched the children at play.

Gonzalez added, "Tomorrow morning, you and Alfredo—we'll meet in my office. Either Alfredo will pick you up on his way or Ana will bring you, OK?"

Faced with a fait accompli, Ken agreed. With that avenue of discussion closed off, he remembered something else he wanted to ask the priest. "Tell me, Father, where did you learn such excellent English?"

Gonzalez grinned: "Boston. If you listen carefully, especially if I speak in a hurry, you can hear traces of my Irish-Catholic immersion come out."

"Why Boston?"

"That's where I went after seminary," he said. "I studied for the priesthood in two Central American seminaries. Then I did some graduate work in Mexico. But my superiors obviously felt they had not inflicted enough pain on me and steered me toward a doctorate in theology. That's how I ended up at Boston University for four years."

Alfredo pointed to the priest's hat, to Gonzalez's obvious embarrassment. "The hat; you ask him," he said, gesturing toward the four-pointed beret Ken had noticed earlier.

"Yes?" he asked.

"You may not have noticed this if you haven't hung around lots of Catholic priests but most of these birettas have only three points," Gonzalez said. "But if you're foolish enough to go on and invest all your time in getting a doctorate, they give you another point. That's it: four years or more of study and that's after the six I spent in seminary and all I get is one more point on my hat," he said with a laugh.

"What was your dissertation on?"

"On Latin American interpretations of the atonement. Fascinating stuff but not much help when you're comforting a dying parishioner or comforting a couple whose daughter has run off to the big city."

Already impressed with this man's winsomeness and grace, Ken wondered how a man of this caliber had ended up in this remote part of the world. So he asked.

"The bishop, the one I was responsible to, he assigned me here. That was twelve years ago. Six little churches and a motorcycle, that's what they gave me. Oh, and a tiny house."

He continued, "The villages are spread out over about a twenty-five-kilometer radius but the poor roads make the distances seem much greater. The bishop has given me the chance a few times to move on, offering me a city parish.

"But I love these people and this place so I'm happy to continue my ministry here. It's not always easy. My people bring into the church an unhealthy legacy of syncretism, borrowing quite often non-Christian ideas from traditional religion. They can be a suspicious bunch too and it's an uphill battle getting them grounded in the traditional Catholic teachings that you'd be more familiar with back home, Ken."

Ken was engrossed.

"Yes, I know you and Alfredo have big doctrinal differences with us Catholics, but if you want to argue about theology with us, let's focus on the actual teachings of the Church and not the beliefs of people like my parishioners, simple folk who—how shall I put it—are not yet thoroughly grounded in Catholic teaching and, to be honest, resist aspects of it. How fair would it be if I lumped all Protestants together, including the snake handlers and the prosperity gospel TV evangelists, who must induce shudders in the Holy Spirit."

He paused, then sighed. "In brief, for all their faults and theological shortcomings, these are my people, and I plan to stay with them, teaching and serving them as best I can, until God clearly tells me to move on."

Then, trying to lighten the mood, he added, "I did a deal a couple of years ago and upgraded from the bike and got a car instead. But the bishop doesn't know."

Alfredo laughed knowingly, tapping his bent forefinger against his temple, as if to say, "I've got the goods on you, my man, in case the bishop ever shows up."

Gonzalez added, "Much, much better for getting around in the rainy weather. On my bike, when I'd get soaked, Alfredo always asked if I'd been to see John the Baptist."

Alfredo burst out laughing.

Gonzalez shook his head in mock sadness and added, "Some of these evangelicals can be terribly cruel, you know."

13

Andre's Next Step

Sunday Afternoon

BACK HOME, THE MOOD in the Borgvik household was far less congenial. Andre fumed unrelentingly about the missing group, ranting about the pastor's, the youth pastor's and the Mission Matchers' incompetence and irresponsibility. His wife, Priscilla, knew he was capable of extended verbal onslaughts about the slightest of grievances. But his rant today had an added dimension of anger.

Then, to her surprise (because his rants were typically only a venting mechanism), this time he spoke of the need "for us to do something." By "us" he of course meant himself.

"I'm going down there to look for them," he told Priscilla.

"Don't be ridiculous, Andre."

Ridiculous though his idea might be, it was clear to Priscilla that Andre's mind was made up. He stood up from the dining room table, having just eaten the last mouthful of pasta that Priscilla had prepared for lunch and proclaimed: "I'm going to look for airfares."

Priscilla knew he was serious; normally he helped to clear the dishes but once he latched on to some new idea he could think of nothing else.

Priscilla sighed and began clearing the table and resigning herself to yet another manifestation of her husband's impetuosity.

14

―――――

Evangelicals vs Catholics

Sunday Afternoon

WITH LUNCH BEHIND THEM, Pastor Alfredo interjected in English, "Isn't there something else we should tell Ken?"

"Yes, yes," Fr. Gonzalez resumed. "We do something else too, when the weather is good. We have a football match, between the Catholic men and the evangelicals. Mostly the young men but whoever we can get."

He turned and spoke to Alfredo in Spanish and they had a brief conversation that Ken correctly guessed had to do with the condition of a field towards which they repeatedly gestured. Ken hadn't consciously noticed the field until now, across the road leading to the church and a couple of hundred yards down the hill he and had walked on the way from her home.

"We play today," Alfredo said enthusiastically. "We'll win this time!"

For the first time Ken saw a divide between the forces of Catholicism and the evangelicals in San Pedro: This soccer rivalry was deeply rooted.

Gonzalez said, "Alfredo likes to think his team is dominant right now. But his assessment is as misguided as his theology."

Alfredo shook his head in mock anger, saying: "No, no; even with Pope they lose."

Ken couldn't help laughing and asked the priest, "Are they going to play today? Will the field be muddy? I noticed the road here was partly muddy."

"Oh it'll be OK; yes, we'll play today," Gonzalez said. Then he asked Alfredo a question, which led the pastor to summon one of the men in his congregation. He asked him something. The conversation got more lively and then Alfredo spoke with Gonzalez. He in turn finally brought Ken into the loop.

"I gather that Alfredo's team is all set to go but their captain, Luis, tells us that our Catholic team is short two players. Luis has just learned that they got stuck on the other side of the bridge and are staying with family in Santa Gabriella. I didn't know that. So maybe we can't play after all."

But then Alfredo became quite animated, chattering to both Luis and Gonzalez on a matter clearly of great importance and complexity. As this burst of exchanges slowed to a conclusion, the priest turned to Ken and said, "Well, we have an answer; Alfredo says that two of the men in your group—maybe you too—will play for the Catholics."

Alfredo and Luis nodded vigorously; both the agenda for the afternoon, and its participants, were decided.

Gonzalez explained, "You see, we have a tradition that if we are short one player, the match can go ahead—but not with two. And you can't have someone from the other side on your team. But you are visitors, guests. And you could play for either team." Then he grinned and added, "So today you are honorary Catholics!"

And so they were. Ken approached his now well-fed flock and explained the situation. "We're guests here," he said. "And we can hardly turn down their invitation—really, more a demand—that we provide them with two players."

He looked at Zach and Bill, as the obvious candidates. The only other boy, Tim, was a known lover of the indoors and things academic, with a total lack of interest in anything athletic. Bill had played soccer for a recreational league. But Zach's game was tennis; he knew only the rudiments of soccer: that you were supposed to kick the ball into the goal and that you couldn't touch it with your hands.

"Bill, Zach: you're it," Ken said.

Kyra spoke up. "Hey Ken, what about the girls? Are we nothing? Sharon's a starter on her school's soccer team, remember?"

Ken did remember but had automatically ruled out any female participation.

"Yeah, I know," he said. "And she could probably run rings around Bill and certainly Zach. But this is a male-dominated society and they've asked for two guys."

"But that's just not right," Kyra said. "We need to show them that girls can be as good as guys, even better, on the field."

"No," Ken responded. "We don't need to show them anything. We're here as their guests, we play by their rules—whether we like them or not." He recalled what he'd learned in his undergraduate days, when he was an exchange student to Botswana. The person in charge of the study abroad office had prepared the outgoing students to expect unwelcome features in the countries where they were to spend a semester, many of them living with a family. "Remember," Ken recalled her words, "they've done these things you don't like for a long, long time and they're going to continue doing them long after you leave. Suck it up. Don't try to change them, because you won't and you can't."

Kyra adopted pout mode, scowling and folding her arms in opposition to Ken's sexism.

He ignored her and turned his attention back to Bill and Zach.

"Well?" he asked.

"I guess," said Bill. And Zach said, "Sure."

Kyra's pout continued.

"OK," Ken said. "I'll go and tell them you'll do it."

"But we don't have any gear—no cleats or shin-guards or anything," Bill said.

"Well, you'll just have to make do with what you have," Ken said. "I suspect they aren't well equipped either."

Ken was right. As the combatants for each side began drifting in, it was clear that this was like a come-as-you-are athletic event. The teams were dressed in a rag-tag array of shorts, long pants, T-shirts and other short-sleeved tops—and typically well-worn shoes. Ken counted at least four players who were barefoot; he shuddered to think what it must be like to play without shoes on the rough, gravelly ground that pretended to be a soccer field.

Zach noted that Bill was wearing a pair of Nikes that must have cost at least $150, possibly more than the annual family income of some of these players. Zach had seen several players on both teams looking enviously at his shoes. He didn't think Bill had noticed.

Alfredo approached and pointed to his wristwatch and raised a finger: "*Una hora*, one hour," he said. "First, we relax," he said, rubbing his stomach, which Ken took to mean the players needed to digest before the showdown. Several of the players, all in their late teens or early twenties (with one exception), were undistinguished by any uniform. As they mingled with Ken's group, some spoke fragmentary English; most did not. But even those who obviously weren't tracking the halting conversations were determined not to miss out on hanging with this group of exotic young women.

Sissy, in her role as chaperone, monitored as best she could both the chatting and behavior, lest any of it slip into serious flirting—which she wouldn't have known how to address even if it occurred.

None did. But at least a handful of youths on each side of the language divide eagerly wished that day they could do two things. One was to speak enough Spanish or English (depending on the person of interest) to deliver a reasonably credible conversation starter. (How might "Did the sun come out or did you just smile at me?" be received? Or would "Well, here I am—what are your other two wishes?" translate culturally?)

The second need was to have something to say beyond whatever opener you used. Anyone could memorize a good pick-up line or two. But the real test lay in one's ability to sustain a basic conversation. Sadly for them, none of these young people could aspire to that level of communication. Several young unilingual males and females that afternoon made solemn but short-lived vows to learn enough English or Spanish so that if a similar opportunity arose in future they would not be limited merely to admiring glances, fleeting smiles, and brief eye contact.

⊙❖⊙

An hour and a half later, with the time now approaching 3 p.m., the Catholic priest and the evangelical pastor summoned the teams to the makeshift field that was to be the site of the impending battle. By gestures, and in some halting English, the Catholic captain lined up Bill and Zach to play defense. Zach didn't care; he didn't particularly know what he was doing anyway. But Bill was miffed. He was accustomed to playing offense but, remembering Ken's words about them being guests, accepted his assignment without spoken complaint.

Gonzalez and Alfredo conferred before summoning the two captains. The four of them spoke briefly, after which the captains shook hands to loud cheers from two lines of spectators: The Catholic supporters lined up on one side of the field, the Protestants on the other.

Bill and Zach took their places with the Catholics. The oldest player on the field was ironically named Juanito, "little John," the Catholic goalie. He stood at least six feet five and appeared to be in his late thirties. He greeted the boys enthusiastically and laughingly said, "You play for us, you now Catholics for life."

Noticing Bill's fancy Nikes, players from both sides resorted to calling him "Señor Nike."

Bill wondered whether Gonzalez or Alfredo would serve as referee and if so, how awkwardly partisan that might be. But neither of them stepped onto the field to fill that role. To Bill's astonishment the Catholic captain placed the ball on the center spot, gave a thumbs up to his team, and with a kick the match was under way—sans referee.

ⷦ

To Bill's further surprise, the entire match was unlike any he'd been part of before. The teams played according to some kind of honor system, which mostly seemed to work well. A few disputes arose about off-sides and whether this tackle or that was fair. But notwithstanding the occasionally intense verbal conflicts, supplemented by supportive shouts from the sidelines, the two teams played a remarkably clean game. Their play was scrappy but fast.

Some unseen mechanism timed each thirty-minute half; the locals just knew when to stop at the half and at the end. Zach didn't have much to do but acquitted himself adequately, with one exception. Without uniforms to distinguish the teams, he once passed the ball by mistake to a Protestant player, who made an excellent break and came close to scoring.

Bill, by contrast, became something of a mini-hero, as a fierce defender who twice stole the ball and set up a good run by the forwards. One of those ended up in a goal, with the team giving due recognition to Bill's role.

The rest of the First Church group were transfixed by the spectacle and found themselves uninhibitedly cheering for Bill, Zach and the Catholics, cheers that may have helped that team move to a 2–0 lead.

Ken wondered what the more conservative members back home at First Church would have made of this afternoon's activities—or more correctly, those members who had never thrown off the strong anti-Catholic bias acquired during their youth. Mostly this wasn't an issue at the church, whose leadership under Pastor Lawrence and his immediate predecessor had cultivated what Ken regarded as "a principled openness" in the church. Some die-hards remained, though, committed to maintaining the centuries-long divide between Protestants and Catholics. He was reminded of the story about the writer and actor, Quentin Crisp. On one occasion he told an audience in Northern Ireland that he was an atheist and a woman stood up and asked him, "Yes, but is it the God of the Catholics or the God of the Protestants in whom you don't believe?"

Ken clearly remembered from his seminary days a course co-taught by a rabbi and a Jesuit, designed to highlight the differences between and similarities among the Jewish, Catholic and Protestant traditions. For Ken the theological gaps between the latter two remained significant. He had strong theological problems with the Catholics' views on the Eucharist as well as what he saw as a less-than-Christocentric focus on Mary. Then there were practices, such as what he saw as an infatuation with relics, for example, that were clearly unbiblical.

Yet he came to admire what he saw as the incredible depth of Catholic theology and church tradition. None of the students in the seminary class came close to out-arguing the Jesuit (or the rabbi, for that matter). Similarly, Ken greatly admired the Catholics' deep commitment to issues of social justice.

Humility compelled him and his fellow seminarians to concede that Protestants were far from cohesive in the theology and faith practice they presented to the world. Indeed, he recalled how the class squirmed when the Jesuit spoke of "the scandal of Protestant disunity." He went on to cite an estimate that there are approaching nearly 50,000 Protestant denominations around the world, depending on how you define a denomination.

The course hadn't come close to converting him either to Judaism or Catholicism, but he emerged with a far greater respect for both traditions, especially the latter. He came to regard the Protestant and Catholic streams of the faith as twins separated at birth, who had then been raised in such different families that—when they miraculously found each other as adults—they would never end up seeing things the same way. Then, Ken wondered, what about the Orthodox branch of the faith? "*Triplets* separated at birth?" he speculated.

The third Catholic goal brought him back to reality.

ৰ৽৹

At the match's conclusion came high-fives and even some hugs among the rivals, which contrasted with the unrelenting flow of jibes, insults and mockery that flowed from the players during the match, and which were paralleled by comparable good-natured abuse from each team's supporters.

Following the match, a plentiful supply of soft drinks and snacks appeared, as the ribbing between the players (all of it lost on the Americans) continued.

Gonzalez, Alfredo and Ken, who had been seated in folding chairs, walked over to the snacks and drinks table, where they had had lunch.

The priest said, "A pretty clean game today. Sometimes the boys get a bit heated, but we've drilled into them that the way they play is to honor the fourteen victims from the war. We emphasize that they are rivals, not enemies, a difference that's sometimes difficult for young people to grasp on the football field, and off."

Then he and Alfredo turned to a woman whom Ken didn't think he'd seen before. She provided each of the three men with a copy of a list showing which of the Americans was staying where.

Alfredo said, "We divided them up more or less with half for each church. Ana said she is happy for you to stay with her, Ken." Ken thought back to Braxton's remark early this morning about the risk was taking in hosting him, and was moved by her generous, risk-taking spirit.

The rest of the list meant little to him as he had no idea who the hosts were. But he was struck by the sensitivity of whoever had done the allocations: mostly the girls were billeted in pairs. The two who were going to be on their own were assigned a female host. In case Ken hadn't noticed this, Gonzalez made a point of making this explicit. Bill and Zach were with a family of five, including a boy a year or so younger than them. Tim was on his own with a young married couple and Sissy with another of the village's widows.

Anticipating Ken's sense of responsibility for his group's well-being, Gonzalez added, "They'll all be safe and in good hands."

⊙⹓⊚

It was now well after 4 p.m. and the light was beginning to fade. Unlike Ken, who had left his belongings in the house, all the others had brought their backpacks to the church. The group members were introduced to their host families. In one or two instances, they were the same people they'd stayed with last night. But most arrangements were new.

After consultation with Gonzalez and Alfredo, Ken told the group that they needed to be back at the church tomorrow at 9. With varying degrees of apprehension at the unknown, the group dispersed to their assigned lodgings.

Ken chatted a bit more with the two men and they agreed they'd meet at the Catholic church's rectory at 8 to plan activities for the group. Ken thanked them and then headed off with Ana, who'd been waiting patiently to escort him back home.

15

Andre's Plan

Sunday Evening

ANDRE BORGVIK WAS OBLIVIOUS to the time. He'd spent the entire afternoon on the computer, searching for:

- Air fares to San Gabriel.
- Car rentals options at the San Gabriel airport.
- Hotels in San Gabriel, for his first night's stay.
- Visa and inoculation requirements, if any, and
- Possible travel insurance options.

He also repeatedly checked news sites for possible plane crashes, relieved each time he found nothing. He also checked in the small safe in the main bedroom and, yes, his passport was there and was current.

When Priscilla brought him some mid-afternoon hot chocolate and cookies she knew better than to tell him to stop being so obsessive. Instead, she committed her energies to frequent and urgent prayer for Heidi's safety, as well as that for the group as a whole.

The only additional word they and the other parents received on Sunday was a text from Pastor Lawrence indicating that despite continuing contacts with Mission Matchers and their on-the-ground man in San Pedro, Ricardo, they had no new information.

Andre had tried to find a US Consulate in San Gabriel, but the closest US outpost was the embassy in the capital, 220 miles away; they would be no help.

By late afternoon Andre decided that come Monday morning he would fly to San Gabriel to learn what apparently nobody else could: discover the whereabouts of his daughter and what, if anything, had befallen her and the First Church group.

He told Priscilla over dinner what he would do. He had already emailed his boss saying a family emergency would keep him out of the office for a few days.

Priscilla knew better than to argue with him or to tell him to wait. Instead, she did some laundry to ensure he had enough clean clothing and then helped him to pack. He planned to take just a carry-on bag and a briefcase containing his laptop and smartphone (which Google had assured him would work in San Gabriel).

"Don't you think you should tell Pastor Lawrence of your plans?" Priscilla asked. "Or at least wait until morning to see if there's any news before buying a ticket?" Still anxious about Heidi, not having heard a word about the group, she knew the group was in God's hands—and she had serious doubts about Andre's willingness to serve as God's self-proclaimed assistant.

"No point. They know nothing more than I do. Anyway, although I've bought the ticket, it can be cancelled for up to twenty-four hours," he said. "So if we get news tonight I can scrap the whole thing. Depending on what news we get, that is. They might still need help down there and then I'd be ready to go."

Priscilla knew Andre was set on doing this. But she still pushed him to phone Pastor Lawrence and let him know of his plan; he grudgingly relented. As both she and Andre expected, the pastor said that this was premature and that he should wait: Monday was a working day and they were more likely to get answers then.

It wasn't enough to dissuade Andre and he told Priscilla that unless some clear explanation came through tonight, he'd leave for the airport at 5:45 tomorrow to begin the three-leg flight to San Gabriel, starting at 6:35. If the connections worked well, he would arrive in San Gabriel in the late afternoon, early enough to do some investigating.

Like Priscilla, Pastor Lawrence knew Andre well enough to realize there was no point trying to talk him out of going; he just hoped Andre wouldn't be fool enough to do so. If he went, the best the pastor could hope for was that he did no harm. And after all, it's his money and time he's spending, the pastor thought. But if there were some crisis with the group, he reflected that Andre Borgvik was one of the last people he'd like to help resolve it. Far better to have as a resource someone like Joachim Estes or Irma Watson, the mom who was supposed to accompany the group but had to drop out because of her mother's heart attack.

But Pastor Lawrence didn't want to think about potential crises. He recalled the saying that "worry is interest paid on trouble before it falls due." No need to worry about what he kept telling himself was almost nothing more than a communication problem.

Andre, though, was gearing up for full crisis mode. He thought of taking his revolver but Priscilla talked him out of it. "You'll never get on the plane with it," she sensibly reminded the man who was planning to take only carry-on luggage. "And they wouldn't welcome it in San Gabriel either," she said. "The last thing they want is an angry Yankee packing heat."

By 9 that night he was packed and ready for an early morning airport ride and, he hoped, prepared too for whatever San Gabriel might present him.

16

Annabel's Unhappy Night

Sunday Evening

ANNABEL'S STOMACH CRAMPS BEGAN at about 9:30, a few hours after the simple dinner her Catholic host mom had prepared. Annabel's initial apprehension about being assigned to one of the Catholic hosts, and on her own, quickly eased as she experienced Cristina's kindness.

Cristina Ortega was a widow; her husband had died twelve years ago. She lived alone after each of her four adult children had moved to the city, the common plight of thousands of older parents and grandparents throughout the country, who were deprived of seeing their grandchildren growing up in front of them. Travel to the city was hard for this seventy-seven-year-old grandmother. Yet she understood why none of her eight grandchildren was genuinely interested in visiting her in a small village that had nothing to offer them. More than once during their infrequent visits she had overheard the pre-teen kids of her son Alberto saying, with the honesty of young children everywhere, "*Es aburrido*—It's boring."

Having this young American guest, someone unrelated but about the same age as some of her grandchildren, was thus an unexpected pleasure—even though this delightful young woman couldn't speak Spanish. With two years of high school French, though, Annabel repeatedly found herself blurting out words and phrases that Cristina thought she was supposed to understand, but didn't.

With her brain getting signals that its owner was in a situation demanding a response in a foreign language, French was the best it could come up with. "Was this Spanish with a bad accent?" Cristina thought, when Annabel repeatedly said "*merci*" or "*merci beaucoup*," for yet another kindness or gestured direction, even though it sounded nothing like "gracias." Or, Cristina thought, perhaps it was an idiomatic thing; maybe this was the Spanish that people spoke in the United States these days.

֍

Cristina had been meticulously careful in preparing the meal. As the assignments for hosting the First Church group were made, Ana—Ken's host—had emphasized how delicate Americans' constitutions were and that every precaution should be taken when preparing food and drink.

However, Annabel's growing intestinal discomfort had nothing to do with Cristina's catering; she was having a delayed reaction to one of the snacks she'd eaten after the soccer. Nor was she alone: Bill, the soccer celebrity of the day, and Sharon were having similar reactions. Sharon had begun erupting a couple of hours earlier. Bill's condition was the mildest of the three but still involving the body's repeated and emphatic responses to an unwelcome intruder, entailing repeated sprints to the outhouse.

Fortunately for Annabel, she and Cristina were succeeding in finding common ground: Cristina was showing her guest family photos in an album. Annabel reciprocated with photos on her phone, which she'd brought despite being told there'd be no signal. This was to serve as her camera, to capture the people of San Pedro and the group's week of mission service.

As her queasiness began and her stomach churning intensified, it was immediately clear to Cristina what was happening. She produced a chamber pot, one that would save Annabel repeated trips to the outhouse twenty yards from the back door. Then, she sat with Annabel for the next six hours, her arm around her shoulders, at times stroking the young girl's increasingly straggly hair. When needed, she helped Annabel onto the pot to relieve her sorely troubled bowels or held the pot when another bout of vomiting was imminent.

After each use she emptied the pot, rinsed it and brought it back for another round. After the first couple of bouts, Annabel no longer felt embarrassed in front of this kindly woman, who had tenderly and matter-of-factly attended to the needs of her guest in a way one couldn't imagine doing back home. Cristina knew the importance of keeping her patient hydrated, providing her with as much bottled water as Annabel could consume.

Each time Annabel threw up Cristina gently wiped the young girl's mouth with a warm cloth. And each time Annabel reflexively murmured, "merci, merci." Despite this girl's odd Spanish, Cristina knew exactly what she meant.

So it was that evening an unexpected and extraordinary bond was formed between a seventeen-year-old high school student and a grandmotherly woman sixty years older, a woman who knew what being alone meant.

Annabel settled down at about 3 a.m., when she gestured to Cristina that she'd like to sleep. The grandmother helped her to bed, tucked her in, and gently kissed her good night on the forehead, whispering "*Duerme bien, querida nieta*"—"sleep well, little grandchild."

17

Andre Heads South

Monday Morning

ANDRE BORGVIK DROVE TO the airport not long after Annabel fell into a deep sleep. She woke late in the morning after Cristina decided not to rouse her. He had heard nothing more about Heidi or the others in the group and was thus committed to going ahead with his plan. Priscilla, sitting beside him in the car, hoped she'd be awake enough to drive back home. She was used to his impulsive ways, like the time when with two days' notice, they went on an impromptu three-week trip to national parks in the West. The trip was marred by Andre's total lack of planning, which on one occasion led to them having to pay $560 for a hotel room at a resort because no park accommodation was available; a three-day delay because of a car problem that should have been resolved before leaving home; and the death of Heidi's two prized goldfish, Yin and Yang, because in the rush of leaving nobody thought of arranging a fish-sitter.

This latest venture, then, didn't take Priscilla by surprise. But endearing though this man was to her—he was after all a good husband and father, and a man of deep faith—she struggled to cope with this side of his personality. She wondered if he was somewhere on the spectrum for obsessive compulsive disorder. When he fixated on something, there was no stopping him. She kissed him goodbye at the departing flights drop-off zone, and now awake enough to drive home safely, did just that.

Andre's journey to San Gabriel was uneventful. At least, until his arrival. Instead of telling the immigration officer that the purpose of his visit was either tourism (which might have been a stretch, given his limited luggage and early return date on his ticket) or business (without going into specifics), he went into a needlessly detailed account of the missing group. The normally sedate official perked up, especially at the implication that his country was in some way responsible for the disappearance of eleven Americans.

He began peppering this intense visitor with more questions, to the point that Andre's tolerance for bureaucrats, and especially foreign bureaucrats, began plummeting fast. Eventually, getting frustrated with the interrogation, he sounded like Paul telling the magistrates in Philippi that he was a Roman citizen, and announced: "Look, I'm an American," as if that should be the end of the matter.

"Yes," sighed the official. "I can tell." He wearily stamped a blank page, authorizing a stay in the country for sixty days, initialed the stamp and glared at Andre. The stamp specified that he was to engage in no paid labor or business dealings. He then returned the passport and said with just a trace of sarcasm, "Welcome to San Gabriel."

18

———

Developments in San Gabriel
Monday Morning

FIRST THING MONDAY RICARDO phoned the San Gabriel Delta office to learn if any flights originating in the United States were due that morning. There were two. He managed to talk the official into confirming for him that the First Church group was on neither flight. He contacted Mission Matchers in Houston to tell his boss, Clara Small, what he'd learned. She said she couldn't reach her contact on Sunday and had left him a message this morning. She hoped to hear back soon.

While they were still discussing possible next steps, Clara said, "Hang on a moment: I've just got an email." She took a moment to read it and then told Ricardo, "Well, good news and bad news. The first is that they indeed boarded their flight as planned and got to Atlanta on time. Their next stop was Miami, again on time. But that's when the bad news comes in. My contact is puzzled because even though they transferred for their final flight onto the regional airline, Excelente, the details aren't showing up in Delta's system. So he can't be sure that they made that flight. He's looking into it."

What neither Clara nor her man at Delta thought to ask was the exact destination, the question John Braxton knew to ask. The Delta man, not a Spanish speaker, had seen "Santa Gabriella" and assumed it was the same airport as Clara cited: "San Gabriel."

Ricardo then phoned Pastor Sanchez at the San Pedro church, now well supplied with about fifty liters of paint, rollers, trays, brushes, tarps.

But no painters. Had the group made it there since their last conversation, somehow by-passing Ricardo, and the pastor just hadn't told him?

"No," came the reply. No sign of them. The pastor then explained that, as they had arranged, the women of the church had been preparing food for a week now, to cater to the visitors' needs. Accommodation was arranged and special services planned, along with the VBS and *las marionetas*, the puppets. That was to be the highlight of the week for the children. No one in Pastor Sanchez's San Pedro could know that the puppets now lay silent and alone in the darkness of the Delta/Excelente unclaimed luggage shed 320 kilometers away.

When Mission Matchers hired Ricardo as their key person for the region, what struck Clara Strong, besides his excellent English and the depth of his faith, was his initiative and problem-solving skills. He was now completing his seventh year with Mission Matchers and had proven himself able to cope with one crisis after another. He oversaw the evacuation of the sixteen-year-old who broke her leg in three places when falling off a ladder, while painting. He ensured swift medical treatment for several other youths who succumbed to a severe virus and were getting dangerously dehydrated. And there was the incident when his diplomatic skills were severely tested. Two mission groups, one from a Lutheran church in Minneapolis and the other some Southern Baptists from Montgomery, Alabama, arrived more or less simultaneously at the village of Calientes Mejor. Each assumed they were to serve the little Presbyterian church that week. (The leader of the group from Minneapolis had originally booked this date a year earlier but then cancelled it with Mission Matchers—and forgotten to note the revised date of a week later.)

The Presbyterian church members viewed with amazement this surfeit of Americans, whom they were certainly not equipped to house. Ricardo resolved what could have been a major ecclesiastical showdown by finding another small church (Methodist) nearby, which was happy to get their church painted—and could host half the visitors even at short notice. Moreover, Ricardo suggested splitting the two groups, so that half the Lutherans worked alongside half the Southern Baptists in each location.

The result was more than just the diplomatic triumph that Ricardo hoped for; two short-term romances blossomed between the Lutheran and

Southern Baptist youths and yet another culminated in a marriage three years later.

But Ricardo had never been responsible for a group that vanished. While he awaited word from Clara's Delta contact about the final leg of the group's flight into San Gabriel, his mind went to the contingency funds at his disposal. Although most of the First Church group's payment to Mission Matchers covered the painting supplies, his salary, the rental of the two vans, and a few other incidentals, every budget contained a 15 percent contingency line for unexpected expenses—like tracking down lost groups.

He ended his call to Sanchez by saying, "Everyone in the church is expecting the painting to get done this week and we don't want to disappoint them. Take the church van and go into Velasquez and pick up three or four day-laborers and get them going on the painting. I'll come and see you later today and I'll pay them the going rate." Velasquez was a small but vibrant market town between San Pedro and San Gabriel, something of a commercial center for the region—and a place where men seeking work would hang out hoping of getting a day's wage, exactly as they had in Jesus' parable of the workers in the vineyard. These men could at least get started on the project while he continued trying to track down those who should have been doing the work.

Ricardo also wondered fleetingly if Sanchez might find in Velazquez's for-hire crowd a competent puppeteer, so as not to disappoint the kids. He thought it unlikely.

19

The Parish Church of San Felipe

Monday Morning

As planned, Ken, Fr. Gonzalez and Pastor Alfredo met at 8 on Monday morning, at the Catholic church. Having grown up in evangelical churches, Ken had experienced minimal contact with Catholics. He'd known a few deeply committed Catholics in college but for the most part his impression (certainly reinforced by his evangelical subculture) was that Catholics needed to be viewed warily. He'd been in only a few Catholic churches before: a couple of cathedrals while visiting France and another back home when his cousin married a Catholic lass (who, to the groom's parents' discomfort, insisted on a Catholic wedding).

So he was prepared for a church replete with what he regarded as garish, even grotesque statues and other artwork. Probably everything would have an over-the-top baroque lavishness. "Baroque was the right term, wasn't it?" he wondered. But whatever the style, he found it off-putting. And he expected a bloodied statue of Jesus on the cross, with a pitiful expression that may have captured the agony of Jesus' crucifixion without even a hint of the resurrection. Then there'd be the candles, the incense, the pomp and ceremony of the priest and his entourage entering like royalty.

So Ken entered with trepidation, but not unprepared, the Church of San Felipe, to which Ana had dutifully accompanied him to ensure he didn't get lost on the four-minute walk from her house. She had fed him well, once again, after he enjoyed an unexpectedly good night's sleep. She gestured for him to go inside and waved goodbye.

He found the interior of the San Felipe parish church as understated as the French cathedrals were overdone. The church was a model of simplicity. Wooden benches, with no backs, provided seating for perhaps fifty people. A central aisle separated the seating, and Ken assumed (correctly) that men sat on the left, women on the right. The altar was made out of a light-colored wood, as was the pulpit. Standing on the altar were what he assumed (again correctly) the chalice and a tray with wafers, ready to be consecrated. At the entrance to the church was a three-foot high stone baptismal font.

But it was the crucifix that most intrigued him. It was a spare carving of a thin Jesus, whose skin color closely resembled that of the light brown skins he'd seen ever since arriving in the country. The crucifix, about five feet tall, was of wood that perfectly matched the altar and the pulpit. It was the expression on Jesus' face, though, that captivated him. To be sure, it reflected the agony he was enduring. But there was something about those brown eyes. They looked as far upwards as his bowed head would permit, with a look of satisfaction or completion. It was as if the eyes were speaking those triumphant words from the cross, "It is finished!"

Ken was enthralled by how something was simultaneously so deceptively simple and powerful. He stared at the crucifix for perhaps two minutes before he realized that Gonzalez had come up behind him.

"Gripping, isn't it?" he said, more of a statement than a question.

"It's amazing," said Ken. "Who made it?"

"An artist in Santa Gabriella. When you go back that way, if you have time look for his small gallery. I'll give you directions."

The priest continued, "My predecessor saw this and wanted to buy it but the artist insisted on making it a gift. It has a powerful impact in Mass, I can assure you. We had only three people at Mass today but when each of them came up for the Eucharist I saw that no matter how many times they've seen it, they once again looked at the image before taking the elements."

At that point Alfredo joined them and Gonzalez led them to his small vestry, which had squeezed into it a leather chair behind a small wooden desk, two white plastic chairs for his guests, and a filing cabinet that looked as if it were fifty years old. In fact, it was; it had found its way to San Pedro from Maryland, donated by a church in Baltimore.

The shelves on either side of a small window held a smattering of books, which Ken could see were mostly in Spanish but with a few English titles. On the bottom shelf was, to Ken's surprise, a Keurig coffee maker.

Noting that the Keurig had caught Ken's eye, Gonzalez responded, "Ah yes, the coffee machine. A cast-off from the bishop. He ended up with three, all gifts from visiting Americans who also brought him packets of Starbucks. That's a bit of an insult when you think of the coffee we grow here. But never mind: Ken, do you want a cup? I already know the pastor's order."

"I'll have a Breakfast Blend, if you have one."

He was in luck.

It was now 8:20 and neither of Ken's companions showed any sign of getting down to business, even though they were all due to reconvene at the pastor's church at 9. Ken thought, "Isn't it a bit too early in the day for a mañana mindset?"

20

Planning the Agenda and an
Unwelcome Introduction

Monday Morning

AT LAST THEY TURNED to the business at hand: identifying tasks that the group could undertake in the time they would remain in the village. It was unclear how long that would be; that depended on when he could contact Ricardo or someone else from Mission Matchers and see if it were still worthwhile to go to their original destination.

Here's what Fr. Gonzalez and Pastor Alfredo came up with as possible tasks:

- Speak English with the children at the local elementary school.
- Play games with the children during recess.
- Weed the school yard.
- Fix the brickwork at the village well.
- Provide some respite care for Victoria Rodriguez, a woman in her sixties who was slowly recovering from a stroke; this would give her daughter some rest.
- Babysit for a mom with three-month old twins, to give her a break.
- Clean the San Felipe church, which Ken had noticed was extremely dusty and had numerous cobwebs on the ceiling.

Ken suggested another idea. How about doing a litter patrol, removing at least some of what he found to be a surprising amount of trash scattered around the village.

"Careful here," said Gonzalez. "That's most likely to be seen as something of an insult. You're telling them, 'We don't like your village as it is—you need to conform to our standards.'" He continued, "How would you like it if I were a guest in your home and said, 'You know, these drapes are really dirty—I'll just pop them in the washing machine.' For us to invite you, say, to clean the church, that's one thing. But for you to tell us what to clean . . . Well, you get the picture."

Ken felt embarrassed. "Well, let's just look at the things you've proposed. Let's run them by the group and see what they'd be interested in."

They finished their coffee and headed to Alfredo's church. As they approached the building, Ken noticed a police vehicle, an olive-green Toyota 4Runner decked out with a couple of impressive aerials, emergency lights, a spotlight, and a large customized front bumper that almost audibly said, "Don't you *dare* mess with me."

Leaning against the vehicle was a uniformed, languid man, broad shouldered and about six feet tall. Ken wondered what the man wanted. The officer watched the First Church group gathering by the church entrance. But while he showed no interest in them, he perked up when he saw Ken, Gonzalez and Alfredo. The pastor and the priest quickened their pace, as if cued to do so by some unseen choreographer and greeted the officer and shook hands with him. Pleasantries appeared to follow. But the tone soon changed, as Ken could tell from the distance he was keeping, about fifteen yards back. An animated conversation ensued, with correspondingly increased gesturing by all three men. Ken had no idea what was happening but by the sound of things it looked ominous.

It was. Gonzalez came over to him, looking worried. "We have a problem, Ken," he said. "Officer Manuel here has been contacted by the immigration officials because it appears that your group doesn't have a permit to be in this jurisdiction. Unfortunately, the permit your people lined up for you applies only to the other San Pedro village, and that province. We're in a different province here."

"What does that mean?" Ken asked.

"Well, Manuel has his good days and his bad days. Sometimes he can be an officious SOB and it seems that today is one of his bad days."

"Which means . . . ?"

"He says he needs to take you in for questioning and that he'll have to check with his superiors on what to do next."

"Can't you explain that this is all a mistake and that we didn't even intend to come here?"

"We've done that but as I said, he can be a snotty-nosed bureaucrat at times. Today is one of his bad days. Maybe tomorrow it'll be a good day and he'll release you . . ."

"What do you mean, 'release me'?" Ken interjected. "Am I under arrest?"

"Let's just say you're being 'detained' until further notice," Gonzalez said. "Look, don't worry, Alfredo and I will go to bat for you. I know the regional police commissioner. And not to worry about the kids and Sissy; we'll look after them and keep them busy. Now, let me introduce you to Officer Manuel."

21

The Group Go to Work and
Their Leader is Detained

Monday Morning

As Fr. Gonzalez and Pastor Alfredo promised, they organized Sissy Simons and the seven students who showed up at church. Cristina sent word through a neighbor that Annabel had had a rough night and needed rest. Same with Sharon. First, though, they had to explain Ken's summary departure in the presence of a police officer. Gonzalez told the group it was nothing to worry about, just some technical immigration thing and that the police officer was being melodramatic. In the wake of this development, everyone forgot about the brief devotional in which Ken had planned to lead the group and their minds went immediately to their assignments.

While some of them were dubious about the priest's explanation for their leader's departure in a police vehicle, they were grateful they had something concrete to do. Bill explained that he was still feeling woozy from the night before; even though he had gotten off more lightly than Annabel and Sharon, he felt he could relapse at any moment. So he was put on light cleaning duties in the San Felipe church, along with Heidi and Kyrstie. Kristen and Kyra were assigned to baby-sit the three-month-old twins, to give their mom a break. And Tim and Zach were to serve as a resource at the elementary school, doing conversational English, as best they could, with the children, and play with them during recess. Finally, Sissy Simons, as the only adult in the labor pool, would go to Mrs. Rodriguez, the stroke victim being cared for by her daughter. Gonzalez and Alfredo wisely concluded that sending Sissy was better than one of the girls—and they rightly assumed that any helper should be a female.

Alfredo told the group that language was a barrier but to remember that "the language of love in action will make up for that," and to do the best they could. Gonzalez said a brief blessing on their day's activities and the First Church volunteers were duly dispatched to their assignments.

Someone representing each of the venues was present and they were introduced to their "day workers," with smiles and hand gestures in abundance.

☙❧

Officer Manuel was, on the face of it, friendly enough. Ken even wondered if he was reluctant to do what he was about to do. He explained in his limited English, "No permit, *si*? You come with me, OK?"

Ken thought that Manuel placing him in handcuffs was a step too far. Being in handcuffs for the first time in his life was sobering enough; being cuffed in front of the young people he was leading was positively humiliating. Manuel seated him on the front passenger seat and didn't bother putting a seatbelt on him, something Ken would have done if he could.

Manuel didn't put on a belt either. They set off, with the radio playing lively music interspersed with high energy ads in Spanish that Ken couldn't understand—but which on a few occasions got Manuel nodding in amusement or even laughing out loud. Ken had forgotten to ask Gonzalez where Manuel was taking him and didn't want to ask that now.

Manuel took out a pack of cigarettes and offered one to Ken, who responded by gesturing a "no thanks" and said, "*gracias*" at the same time. Manuel shrugged and lit up, filling the cabin with smoke. They drove for about thirty minutes over often awful, muddy roads, on which Manuel was clearly well practiced.

They arrived at another village, similar in size to San Pedro. They approached what was clearly an official building, with a large radio antenna on its roof, competing for dominance with a tall flagpole that hosted the national flag.

By now Ken needed the bathroom, a need aggravated by the cup of Keurig. As Manuel opened the door for him, he told the officer, "*El baño, por favor*."

"*Si, si,*" said the officer. "*Yo también*—me too," he said, as if he were glad to be reminded of something he'd otherwise forget to take care of.

He unlocked Ken's handcuffs and beckoned him to follow. They entered the police station and Manuel enthusiastically greeted a geriatric uniformed officer behind the desk, who appeared neither to hear nor care about Manuel's greeting; he also showed no interest in the prisoner walking behind him. A TV set and what looked like an antiquated police radio sat on a counter against the back wall.

The two men stood at the urinal, Ken wondering how this day would play out, while Manuel whistled cheerfully as he emptied a prodigiously large bladder. There was a sink to wash their hands but Manuel ignored it. Ken understood why when he turned on the tap; there was no water.

The police officer took him to a cell and almost politely ushered him in. Ken got the impression that Manuel was secretly honored to have such a distinguished, even exotic guest in his jail. The cell had a narrow metal bed with what he was sure was a filthy blanket. Manuel patted Ken's trousers, touching his wallet, signaling for Ken to hand it over. And his watch too. "Talk about a shakedown," Ken thought. But as he watched, the officer put them in a desk drawer, which he then locked. He returned to the cell, gave Ken a thumbs up, and locked him in.

Ken sat on the bed, having moved the blanket to the side. In the corner was a bucket, the purpose of which was immediately evident from the smell. One cell adjoined his, which he assumed was empty because he had neither heard nor seen an occupant. Gonzalez had said the officer wanted to question him about the permit situation. But so far there was no sign of Manuel wanting to do that; nor did Ken think the man, with his minimal English, could do so effectively. The other officer certainly appeared to be out of the picture. Might Manuel be waiting for another police officer, or someone from the immigration service, to arrive? In this culture, where Ken thought nothing happened in a hurry, or even on time, Ken feared it could be days before anyone showed up.

On the one hand, as he recalled Gonzalez's worried demeanor when he explained why Ken was being detained, he found himself veering toward despair at his plight. On the other, he unswervingly believed that his circumstances were in God's hands. He kept reminding himself that if obeying God had brought him to this cell, continuing to obey God would get him out. But what was God expecting of him now, other than a reliance on prayer alone?

Then he wondered about the possibility of Manuel suggesting that with a modest payment, they could resolve everything. He had not anticipated the possibility of an ethical dilemma in which he might have to hand over a bribe—something he was implacably opposed to in principle. Yet what if this were the most responsible course open to him, allowing him to rejoin the group and continue the mission trip unhindered? And if Manuel, or another more senior (and no doubt more expensive) official wanted a bribe, would he have enough cash to buy his freedom? What if he had to pay off multiple parties?

Right now, he felt hopelessly inadequate as the group's leader. Not only had he brought them to the wrong place, now he had allowed himself to be separated from his charges. He was confident that they were in the good hands of two godly men. Meanwhile, he was grateful for what he saw as humane treatment by Manuel, at least so far. Then, he realized, Manuel might just be playing "good cop," waiting for the arrival of the "bad cop" in the next act of this surreal play in which he found himself.

ॐ

He struggled to make sense of how God had allowed this mission trip to stumble from one catastrophe to another. All Ken's planning, all his attention to detail, had now collapsed. His mission trip, he saw, had fallen to pieces. And he now recognized, with embarrassment, his overriding mistake: he had seen this venture as *his* trip, rather than God's. Ashamed, he confronted himself with the reality that he had far more of an ego-investment in this venture than he had realized. Whatever outcomes he had publicly stated he wanted for the week, as much as anything he wanted the group, the church council, Pastor Lawrence, and the congregation to pat him on the back, acknowledging with gratitude his ground-breaking (and successful) trip. No longer. God had allowed the trip to be turned on its head, leaving Ken's ego severely dented.

Far from the cohesive whole that he wanted the trip to be, with the daily vacation Bible school, for example, running seamlessly through the week, the group's possible contributions were now doomed to a fragmented patchwork of disconnected "bits of aspiring helpfulness."

As he tried to pray, he found himself overwhelmed by a flood of doubts, anger and confusion. Without consciously deciding to do so, he found himself praying over and over the Jesus prayer, "Lord Jesus Christ, Son of God, have mercy on me, a sinner."

22

Meanwhile, Back Home

Monday Morning

HAVING HEARD FROM RICARDO, in San Gabriel, and Clara in Mission Matchers in Houston, Pastor Lawrence phoned the travel agent, Libby Waverley, to tell her of the missing group and to learn whatever she could find. He got through to her immediately and discovered that she was already aware of the problem. She had listened to a message from Andre, who had—to the pastor's surprise—already left for San Gabriel to find the group and phoned Libby during his connection in Chicago. He asked her to phone him if there were any updates.

A moment's reflection told him that, out of everyone in the church, Andre was the most likely to have gone off on a spur of the moment adventure. He didn't know whether to admire the man's initiative or deplore his jumping into a quest for which he was temperamentally ill-equipped if he encountered any significant difficulties. "Mr. Diplomacy" he was not and the pastor was uncomfortable at the prospect of Andre representing the church in any way. "The man didn't even have the courtesy to tell me what he planned to do," Lawrence thought.

Libby interrupted the pastor's thoughts about Andre by saying, "I've done a little digging and confirmed what we already know: that the group left here on time, and also connected on time through Atlanta and then in Miami. So I can't understand why they apparently didn't arrive in San Gabriel."

Lawrence muttered to himself, "There was no '*apparently*' to it; they didn't show up—end of story."

She continued, "Let me do a little more research and I'll get back to you. I'll also phone Andre to let him know I got his message."

As promised, Pastor Lawrence then phoned all the parents of the group members, to reassure them that he was actively "working the problem," to use a piece of jargon from his days in the corporate world before being called into full-time ministry twelve years earlier. He decided not to tell any of them about Andre heading toward San Gabriel. Given the often-fraught relationships Andre had with other church members, the pastor didn't want to needlessly stress already worried parents by letting the "Andre dimension" heighten their anxiety.

Well aware that he still needed to finalize arrangements for the Connie Hardman memorial service that afternoon, he began the round of phone calls.

23

Libby Waverley's Unhappy Discovery
Monday Morning

WHEN LIBBY WAVERLEY, THE travel agent, discovered what she had done, she was mortified. She had made mistakes in previous bookings, but nothing of this magnitude—nor for this many passengers.

Two things distressed her about the implication of her error. The first was that nobody knew where the group was. She confirmed that they had landed at Santa Gabriella but apparently nobody knew where they had gone next. She learned too that their luggage was still at the airport.

The second thing that distressed her was that she couldn't imagine how she could right this wrong. Hers was a small travel agency, with just enough profit to pay herself a modest salary and even more modest ones to her two employees. The possibility of refunding commissions to the group came to mind immediately; that was probably the least she could do. But her cash flow couldn't countenance the idea of full refunds to the group; that money had long gone to Delta. She knew she'd have to work on some kind of compensation later.

For now, though, she needed to let Pastor Lawrence know what had happened. So she did, mixing her factual explanation with a barrage of apologies. She got through the conversation, immensely grateful that Pastor Lawrence chose to put a positive spin on the news rather than tear her to shreds.

"Well, we now know they made it and weren't kidnapped by aliens from the planet Zalkony," he said. "Mystery part one is now solved," he added.

"You've done your bit, Libby. Now I guess it's up to us to see how we can solve part two. And Libby, don't be too hard on yourself. This was an understandable mistake. Those names are so close, aren't they? The parents will be relieved to know we have some answers."

He said goodbye, knowing he needed to get back to his list of parents' phone numbers for the second time that morning. His preparations for the Connie Hardman memorial service later today would have to wait yet again. First, though, he needed to call Ricardo.

Libby hung up and raced to the bathroom, fearing that she needed to vomit. After a series of dry heaves she sat on the toilet for a full twelve minutes, reflecting on her blunder, before returning to her desk and telling her two colleagues what had happened.

24

Ricardo Responds
Monday Morning

PASTOR LAWRENCE REACHED RICARDO just after 10, San Pedro time, which was an hour ahead. They didn't speak for long but Ricardo assured the pastor that Libby's explanation made perfect sense. Ricardo said he wanted to speak with Clara at Mission Matchers to look at their options, which included the possibility of him going to Santa Gabriella to track down the group from where they entered the country.

That was in fact the course that Clara and Ricardo agreed on. He would leave as soon as possible for the 300-plus kilometer drive to Santa Gabriella, the other side of the mountains. The entire road was paved and fortunately unlikely to have been affected by the recent heavy rains. However, much of the drive was over the mountains and could be slow going. The road was part of the main east-west national highway but it was only two lanes all the way, which often led to congestion aggravated by slow-moving trucks, especially over the mountain passes. Seeing it was already mid-morning for Ricardo, he told Clara that he thought he could get to Santa Gabriella by late afternoon or early evening, depending on traffic.

Before setting out, Ricardo called Pastor Sanchez in San Pedro to tell him not to expect the First Church group today, and probably not tomorrow either, at the earliest. Then he recalled his earlier promise to show up with funds to pay the casual laborers for today's painting but that wouldn't be possible today. Did Sanchez have enough cash on hand to take care of that?

"Yes, not a problem. And depending on how well they work, I'll bring them back tomorrow," Sanchez said.

With this arrangement in place, Ricardo now prepared for the journey to Santa Gabriella. He'd have ample time en route to plan his strategy. He topped up his battered but faithful Ford pickup with gas; bought a sandwich and a couple of bottles of water at the gas station; and phoned his wife to tell her the latest development in the saga of the missing Americans (unlike many of his countrymen, he refused to call them "gringos") and let her know that he wouldn't be home tonight. Then he left San Gabriel, pulling onto highway 101, well aware that the 15 percent contingency amount in the group's budget was shrinking fast. No matter. Clara had said, "Just do what you need to do. We'll worry about the money later."

25

God is Merciful

Monday Afternoon

KEN LAY DOWN ON the metal bunk and tried to take stock of his situation. He must have fallen asleep, despite the hardness of the bed. He awoke to the sound of the TV: it was blaring a Spanish commentary on a football match between Manchester United and Real Madrid, a delayed broadcast given the time difference with Europe. Fortunately, he could easily see the TV, which was directly opposite his cell. Also watching were Officer Manuel and his colleague, for whom the match had erased his former lethargy.

The match had not been under way for long when Real Madrid scored off a corner, with a perfect header. As if it were rehearsed, the two officers and Ken simultaneously let out an approving yell. Surprised to hear his prisoner's cheer, Manuel turned around and saw Ken watching. He then got up, placed another office chair in front of the TV, and unlocked the cell before beckoning Ken to be seated.

Then, taking his unexpected hospitality to another level, he asked Ken, "You want *cerveza*—beer?" Though not normally a beer drinker, Ken said to himself, "Why not? This is surreal: I'm in jail in a foreign country, watching soccer, and I'm being offered beer by my jailor." Manuel went to a small fridge Ken had not noticed before and grabbed two beers. Ken didn't recognize the brand but that didn't matter; he hadn't eaten or had anything to drink for several hours and was grateful for anything to remedy that. He drank the beer slowly, not wanting to get light-headed. Not only did he seldom drink beer, he never drank on an empty stomach and didn't want any unpleasant and unintended consequences.

Real Madrid and Manchester United kept them entertained for nearly two hours, during which nothing else of note occurred in the police station. Real Madrid won 2–1, to the satisfaction of all three men. (For reasons too complicated to go into here, Ken had never been a Manchester United fan and was glad to see them lose.)

Then Officer No. Two tugged on Ken's shirt sleeve and beckoned him back to the cell. Clearly, this was far from a high security prison; nor were they treating him as a high-risk prisoner. A few minutes later a middle-aged woman arrived, who Ken concluded was Manuel's wife. She carried a covered plate of food (beans, rice and some unidentifiable green vegetable) and an unopened 350 ml. bottle of Coke. Manuel opened the bottle, handed Ken the Coke through the bars, and slid the food under the bottom of the door.

Ken waved to the bearer of his meal and said, "*Muchas gracias.*" During his lunch he heard some static on the radio, followed by a message in Spanish. He couldn't understand it but could pick out a few words like "*Americanos, iglesia*, and Barker (pronounced "Burrka")—Americans, church, and his name.

A few minutes after Ken had finished eating, Manuel unlocked the cell door and beckoned him to the table. He presented Ken with a brief handwritten document and a pen and motioned for him to sign at the bottom. Ken tried to read the few sentences, which ended with his name. But he had no idea what he was expected to sign. Nevertheless, feeling he had no choice, and not wanting to risk annoying or alienating Manuel, he did what the officer asked.

Manuel obviously thought Ken had made the right choice and he smiled broadly. He unlocked the desk drawer and retrieved Ken's wallet and watch, and handed them to him. Then he said, "Now we go," signaling for him to join him outside and get back in the Toyota.

26

Liberation

Monday Afternoon

OFFICER MANUEL AND KEN, now uncuffed, drove mostly in silence back to San Pedro. Now and again they attempted to discuss some aspect of the Manchester United vs Real Madrid match but their language limitations precluded any meaningful post-game analysis.

He didn't know what he had signed but he assumed it had secured his release. He also assumed that the radio message that Manuel received was an instruction from some superior telling him what to do with Ken. He may have admitted to being a human trafficker or a weapons smuggler for all he knew, although from Manuel's demeanor that seemed unlikely. He assumed serious criminals wouldn't be released after signing some informal scratchings on a piece of paper.

Then he checked his assumption; maybe he wasn't being released at all. What if Manuel was driving him to some central prison, where his very presence was hidden from US consular authorities until a full confession was tortured out of him? Maybe it was because Ken had shown no inclination to escape that Manuel was treating him so casually, more like a hitch-hiker he'd picked up on his rounds, rather than some dangerous threat to state security. Was Ken truly being driven to his freedom and a reunion with his group? He thought they were heading back the way they'd come but he couldn't be sure. The countryside appeared much the same wherever you looked. Then again, they could be heading through San Pedro, on to a regional jail in Santa Gabriella.

His musings were interrupted when Manuel switched on the radio, which again blurted the same kind of lively music that they'd listened to earlier that day. If anything, it was even louder than before but not enough to stifle Ken's unspoken prayer, "Lord Jesus Christ, Son of God, have mercy on me, a sinner." Even if he prayed aloud, he wondered if God might struggle to hear him over the blasting radio.

❦

God's mercy was affirmed yet again in Ken Barker's life when early that afternoon Manuel pulled up outside the parish church of San Felipe. He motioned for Ken to remain in the Toyota while he went inside. He and Fr. Gonzalez emerged after about five minutes, both men laughing and with the priest's arm resting companionably on the officer's shoulder.

"Welcome back from your little adventure," Gonzalez jokingly greeted Ken, beckoning him to exit the 4Runner. Manuel shook hands with the priest and turned to shake Ken's hand too. He said, "*Real Madrid, si!*" choosing to focus on the part of their time together that he hoped Ken would find most positive.

Ken grinned, and said, "*Si!*"

"Come inside and I'll bring you up to date," Gonzalez said, as they waved their goodbyes to the departing Manuel. "Let's get you some coffee, too," he added.

The short version was that someone in the regional office at the *Oficina Nacional de Servicios de Inmigración,* or ONSI, (National Bureau of Immigration Services) had phoned Manuel and told him to take the leader of the unauthorized American group into custody for questioning. As a routine matter, the passport officer who had processed the group at the airport had notified his immigration colleagues that a group of American missionaries had arrived and were heading to San Pedro. He assumed, as was normal practice, that Mission Matchers would have obtained the permit the group needed. Ken hadn't noticed the passport official making a note of this, an anomaly that he reported the next day.

An alert colleague of his in the regional office picked up on the missing permit and set things in motion. However, as Gonzalez explained, even though Manuel could be a self-important bureaucrat, he was neither the most diligent nor energetic member of the country's police force. He had never heard the advice of Pope John XXIII: "See everything, overlook a lot, correct a little." But that captured perfectly his philosophy of policing. As long as people on his turf didn't go out of their way to provoke him or do anything manifestly illegal, he in turn wasn't looking for trouble. Or paperwork.

He had done his duty by detaining Ken and reported to the ONSI officials that despite the lack of a permit, he had, following extensive interrogation of the group leader, a Mr. Kendall Barker, and local church leaders, determined that the American group was indeed engaged in legitimate missionary activity. In his professional judgment, therefore, no further action was required. He had, following his superior's instructions (in the radio message that Ken overheard), secured a statement from the foreign national assuring the authorities of the group's missionary intent, and promising they would engage in no paid labor or business activities, which were not allowed by their visas.

Relieved to learn he had not confessed to any heinous crime, and amused at Manuel's self-serving and inflated account of events, Ken chuckled at his good fortune in having been detained by Manuel rather than someone else. It could have been much worse.

"Well, let's put that chapter behind us, shall we," Gonzalez said. "He won't bother us again." He then brought Ken up to date on the group's assignments for the day. Most of the students and Sissy would soon finish their tasks and go to their hosts for the evening. Which brought the priest to his invitation: "I've spoken with Ana and you are having dinner with me tonight. John Braxton will join us. Unfortunately, Alfredo isn't free, so it'll be just the three of us. How does that sound?"

Before Ken could answer, he added, "You know your way now so you won't need an escort. Is 7 OK with you?"

Ken couldn't quite tell if this was an invitation or a command. But he didn't mind. He was honored that the priest had invited him and he also wanted to get to know Braxton better. This time Ken would have a better sense of what to expect from the man. And, to be honest, he'd welcome an evening of stimulating conversation.

27

Andre Tries to Drive a Stick Shift

Monday Afternoon

AFTER CLEARING THE AIRPORT, Andre made his way to the Avis car rental office, a small building that housed three other rental companies, none of whose names he recognized. The sedan he had booked was ready for him. The agent encouraged him to upgrade to an automatic transmission four-wheel-drive, which he said, in excellent English, was a good option as some of the local roads were in poor condition after the recent flooding. He needn't have said "after the flooding" as their condition ranged from poor in the best of seasons, to atrocious in the worst.

Suspicious of being taken advantage of, Andre chose to stick with the sedan: a late model Nissan Versa. He asked directions to the airport hotel he had booked and which he intended to be his base. The agent gave him a basic map of the San Gabriel area. Andre had also printed up his own supply of maps the previous afternoon, including the location of San Pedro. The distance was only sixty kilometers, which he was confident he could cover in under an hour—unaware of what Ricardo had told Ken about it being a ninety-minute trip, given the poor roads. Still, he had no plans to go there this evening. That was tomorrow's task. First, he needed to learn what he could at the airport.

He locked his overnight bag in the trunk of the car and walked back across the road to the airport terminal. It was just before 4 p.m. and people should still be at work, he assumed. He easily found a Delta counter and the pleasant but rather clueless agent didn't understand what he wanted.

She called her supervisor from a back office, who was the model of charm and efficiency.

As he described his mission, Andre saw a knowing expression grow on the man's face. He waited for a pause in Andre's well-rehearsed little speech before holding up a hand and saying, "Yes, I am aware of this situation. We had numerous questions about your group yesterday and today. I can assure you that no groups with any of those names have come through here—on Saturday, Sunday or today. I have here the manifests for each of our flights, and that of our partner airline, Excelente, and there's nothing."

Even though it was a breach of company policy he offered to show Andre the manifests of the relevant eleven US-originating flights. Not that Andre distrusted the man but he wanted to assure himself. He looked over the documents for several minutes, confirming what the man had told him.

Andre had half expected this outcome but he wasn't yet ready to leave, especially not with someone this helpful at his service. "Can you think of anything that might have happened? Any explanation? Were any of your flights diverted because of weather?"

"Not that I know of. But here's a thought," said the supervisor, who'd been with Delta/Excelente for seventeen years and had seen it all. "Have you considered the possibility that they flew to Santa Gabriella? We have the occasional mix-ups because the airports' names are so similar. That's something you might want to check."

"Is it possible for you to look at those manifests, to see if they arrived there?"

No, the system didn't allow for that, sorry. Andre thanked the man, grateful for a possible lead. He returned to his rental car and, after studying the map carefully, prepared to head to his hotel. That's when he realized the Sentra had a stick shift. Like most Americans, Andre had never driven anything except automatics. He sighed, got out of the car and returned to the Avis office to get that automatic four-wheel-drive vehicle. The office was closed. Then he recalled the agent mentioning in his chatty style that Andre was his last customer of the day and that he'd soon head home.

Facing reality, Andre struggled with the lower gears, often stalling in first as he tried to figure out this strange thing called a clutch. Then he kangaroo-hopped the car out of the rental parking lot, as he tried to discover the optimal relationship between the accelerator and the clutch. An airport worker who was corralling luggage carts saw Andre's jerking, lurching vehicle, and chuckled knowingly to himself, "*Americano!*"

With only one wrong turn, and half a dozen cuss words at the drivers behind him who honked when he repeatedly stalled the car at traffic lights, he got to his hotel in twenty minutes, despite the traffic.

Settled in his room, he phoned Priscilla to tell her of his safe arrival. That's when he learned about Libby Waverley's mistake in sending the group to the wrong airport. It confirmed the "Santa Gabriella hypothesis" the Delta supervisor had suggested. He told Priscilla that he'd rented a car and that instead of going to San Pedro he would now head to Santa Gabriella tomorrow "to try and pick up the trail," as he put it.

He also phoned Libby's office, to tell her the same thing and to learn if there were anything new she had found out. He got a recorded message, saying the office was closed and that they'd re-open on Tuesday morning at 8 a.m. He left his information and, taking his phone with him, went in search of dinner.

28

———

The Theft

Monday Afternoon

THAT EVENING, SHORTLY AFTER Ken arrived at the house in time to relax for a couple of hours before dinner, Bill and Zach came to the house. They were staying with a family who were members of the evangelical church. Clearly troubled, they asked if they could speak with Ken, outside.

They told him that when they got back from their day's assignments they noticed their bags and other items had been moved. When they checked more carefully, Bill realized that his Nikes were missing. When they looked in their wallets, which they hadn't expected to need during the day, most of their cash was gone; $60 from Bill (three $20s), and $50 from Zach (two $20s and a $10). The thief had left a few single dollar bills and the change.

"We didn't tell anyone but tried to pretend everything was normal," Zach said. "We told them as best we could that we needed to speak to you about something and they told us where the house was."

"You're absolutely certain about this?" Ken asked.

"Absolutely," was the boys' chorused response.

"And you've told nobody else about this?" Ken asked.

"Nobody," said Bill. "This is really awkward. I mean, this was our spending money for when we go into the city, you know. And they're all so nice, I can't believe anyone in the family would have taken the money."

"Or Bill's shoes," said Zach.

"Did you do a thorough check to see if anything else is missing?"

"Well, not all that thorough but we did go through our stuff and didn't notice that anything else was gone," Bill said. "Our passports are still there and so are my meds. Everything else seemed to be OK."

Ken's detention, jailing and subsequent release were still weighing on him and this latest development pushed him past his limit: "Oh shit," he said. "That's all we need." He added, "Uh, sorry guys, that slipped out."

It was alright; they were not only familiar with the word, they could easily have expressed the same sentiment.

Ken said, "I'll speak to the pastor about this. I know he's not available this evening so it'll have to be tomorrow." He continued, "Look, I'm really sorry about this. Do you have any idea who might have taken the Nikes and the cash? How many people are in the family?"

Zach said, "Well, like Bill said, they're all so nice; I can't believe one of them would have done this. There's the mom and dad, and three kids. One of them was on the soccer team yesterday, Mario. He's sixteen, I think. And there's an older daughter—I don't remember all their names—she's about twenty. And the youngest daughter is maybe twelve or thirteen."

"Gee, this is too bad. I'm really sorry guys," Ken repeated. "But go back home and pretend everything is normal. Don't mention anything to the mom or dad, or the kids, obviously. I'll speak to the pastor tomorrow, as I said, and we'll see what we can do."

They told him they had their wallets with them now. Ken responded, "Good; be sure to keep them with you tomorrow. And bring me your passports tomorrow; I'll hang on to them. I don't think they're at risk; they're of no value to someone in this small village. But let's be careful and I'll look after them for you."

He patted each of them on their shoulders and sent them on their way. "What a bummer," he thought. "Here we have a family showing Christian hospitality to strangers and one of them takes advantage of their guests."

He was not looking forward to the delicate conversation with Pastor Alfredo tomorrow. Nor, he knew, would the pastor look forward to his conversation with Bill and Zach's family, and—assuming one of the kids was the culprit—the shame it would bring on that mom and dad.

29

——

Dinner

Monday Evening

KEN DECIDED NOT TO mention the theft at dinner; that was a conversation he needed to have with Pastor Alfredo. The priest's home, a modest concrete block house with a small but neatly maintained vegetable garden, adjoined the church and so was easy to find. The priest's housekeeper met Ken at the door. An uncharacteristically tall woman, nearly six feet, Lucy had a gaunt, even cadaverous resting face, with a haunted look. Yet it lit up upon seeing Ken, revealing a mouth devoid of a sizeable proportion of its original teeth but which nevertheless yielded a joyous and welcoming smile. She muttered something in energetic Spanish, beckoning him to enter.

Lucy, he was to learn, spoke not a word of English. But as he was also to discover during the course of a two-and-a-half-hour meal, she was a superlative cook. Equally surprising was the menu. Far from the ubiquitous rice and beans combinations that he kept encountering, the leisurely paced three-course meal consisted of asparagus soup, roasted chicken with a range of home-grown vegetables (as Fr. Gonzalez proudly confirmed), and a magnificent peach pie with genuine cream. Where Lucy had obtained the ingredients remained a mystery. But he thought if Catholic priests routinely ate like this, even in rural Central America, he might be tempted to pursue holy orders.

As the evening began to wind down, at 9:30, Ken found himself suddenly drowsy—and thus all the more grateful for the two cups of coffee that culminated the meal. He declined the priest's offer of a brandy, which Braxton had unhesitatingly accepted.

The evening had begun with a glass of imported Portuguese sherry, a first for Ken, whose alcoholic intake back home was minimal. Taking his cues from Gonzalez and Braxton, he too sipped his beverage as they eased into wide-ranging conversation.

Ken thought of the humbler fare the kids and Sissy were no doubt eating tonight and wondered how guilty he ought to feel at receiving such pampering. He told himself that such guilt was part of the price of leadership, a price he was willing to pay.

The conversation began with Braxton asking for an update on Ken's encounter with Officer Manuel. Gonzalez added some details on the back story. He had planned to phone Manuel's superior, who was based in Santa Gabriella, to vouch for Ken and the group. But that would have entailed driving at least half-way into town, something he expected might be possible only tomorrow, Tuesday, at the earliest. Still, that was all moot now.

That led Ken to ask, "How will we know when communication will again be possible?"

"That's pretty easy," said Braxton, who was a much mellower version of the man Ken had met the previous morning. "We can usually tell by the uptick in traffic coming through the village; you will have noticed no trucks today. The few cars you might have seen today belong to the few locals who can afford them. But the trucks are a sure signal that the bridge is open again. And one just needs to get about ten K's the other side of the bridge before you can pick up a signal."

Ken then shared a thought that he'd had only after Manuel had dropped him back in San Pedro. "I wonder if I could have used his radio to call out and let our people back home know what's happened—and also our mission group contacts here."

Gonzalez responded. "Probably would have been a bad idea to try. Manuel can be loosey goosey about a lot of stuff but they're incredibly strict about using the radio only for police business. He wouldn't have let you, even under the best of circumstances." He continued: "And remember you were his prisoner, so he'd hardly want his bosses knowing he'd allowed someone who should have been in the cell using police communications for personal reasons. No, all things considered, don't think this was a missed opportunity."

Braxton followed up Ken's train of thought: "Look, depending on what we see tomorrow, maybe I can get you to the other side of the bridge and see if you can call out."

"You have a car?" Ken asked, not having noticed a second vehicle parked alongside the priest's well-worn Peugeot 207.

"No, a motorcycle."

"Ah," said Ken, noncommittally. He had a thing about motorcycles, after one of his best friends from seminary was killed by a hit-and-run driver, two years into his first pastoral call. "And on these roads . . ." he thought. But he didn't see how he could turn down Braxton's offer.

"Thanks, that would be great," he said.

⚬⚬

"Well, that's taken care of," Gonzalez said. "What I want to hear, Ken, is something about your theology of mission. And how does that tie in with best practices for economic development? I assume you see a close link between those two in a country like ours, yes?"

What was this: an oral exam in seminary? He glanced at Braxton, whose eyes Ken thought had acquired a mischievous twinkle. Gonzalez wasn't exactly looking smug but he exuded an obvious satisfaction with his question.

Had they planned this as an intellectual mugging? Ken wondered.

"Well, um . . ." he began, trying to get his mind into gear.

"Take your time," Gonzalez said, helping himself to some more roast chicken. "Any more for you, John, Ken? There's plenty; don't be shy."

Here he was, facing two men, a priest with a doctorate in theology and an acerbic critic of missions, and he was expected after a grueling day to provide an impromptu discourse on missions and economic development. If he didn't like Gonzalez as much as he did, he would have resented being set up like this.

"As far as missions go," he began, "I think Christians have a clear biblical mandate, based on the Great Commission, in Matthew 28. To go into all nations and make disciples, right?"

"Go on," said the priest.

"Well, making or rather winning disciples comes in various forms. There's plain evangelism, where you present the gospel message. And there are other mission activities that go along with that, like health care and education. I mean, Protestants and Catholics alike are legendary for their outreach with hospitals and schools and universities and so on."

99

"What about development?" Braxton interjected. "What responsibilities does the church have in countries like this?"

"Well, sure. Christians need to be alert to, responsive to basic needs: hunger, health care, sanitation, all that kind of thing," Ken replied, feeling he was grasping.

Braxton responded: "So missionaries like your group should meet people's emergency needs? Like those following natural disasters: floods, earthquakes, famine, that sort of thing?"

"Yes, of course," Ken said, wondering where Braxton was taking this.

"Would you define that kind of missionary help as 'mercy help,' which literally helps people stay alive?" asked Gonzalez.

"Yes, you could call it that."

Gonzalez asked, "What about the four suitcases of children's clothing I understand your group brought, but are now presumably sitting at the airport? Does that fall into the 'mercy help' category? Are you meeting an immediate, life-saving need with the clothing?"

"Well, no," said Ken, again feeling he was being set up. "But this will greatly help those families we expected to meet, whose poverty makes it hard for them to afford clothing."

"What do you think Mrs. Fernández will think of your plan?" asked Braxton.

"Who?"

"Mrs. Fernández; she lives in the village and makes a meager living by trading in good second-hand clothing, for adults and kids," Braxton elaborated. "Those four suitcases, if their contents are unleashed on this village, will flood the market and make her business redundant—at least for kids' clothing."

Braxton continued: "You see, the problem with churches and other charities is this: they love to help in crises. It's both easy, at least comparatively, and immediately gratifying. You can say we shipped so many tons of food to people in the famine area and you estimate how many lives you've saved." He continued: "You feel good about yourselves, and I suppose you're entitled to; you've actually saved human lives by your actions and that's great.

"But where are all these do-gooders when the flood waters have subsided, or the aftershocks from the earthquakes have ended and there's nobody left to be rescued, or when food supplies have stabilized and people no longer need those food packages?"

The needs have shifted to rebuilding and re-establishing their communities, Braxton said. "They no longer need emergency supplies of blankets or medicines or food. The emergency is over. Now they need support for the long haul and that's not nearly as sexy." He added, "And for that kind of help, you need specialized people. None of your people have training in economic development, do they?"

Ken wanted to say, "They're just high-school kids, damn it." But he realized that would simply prove Braxton's point. Instead, he said, rather lamely, "There's nothing we can do about society-wide problems. We think God wants us to do the little we can, and he will multiply the results."

Braxton nodded an acknowledgement of this truism but resumed his argument: "As I said to you yesterday, communities like this can always use some good medical care. We'd welcome a clinic or two. But without sounding ungrateful for the sacrifices I know your group made to get here, we simply don't need puppet shows and used children's clothing nearly as much as we need improved crops and education for kids of all ages. Do you know that in this country most rural kids never get beyond grade 5?"

Ken didn't.

"Not much better in the urban areas either; most are gone by grade 8 so nationally only a pitiful fraction of kids complete high school," Braxton added.

Gonzalez jumped into the discussion or, as Ken perceived it, the grilling.

"Ken, let me notch it up to another level. We Christians should *of course* be engaging in acts of mercy, the kind John described. But is there much point providing only vacation Bible schools to people who are tenant farmers who have to turn over half their crop to landlords? These people are trapped in a cycle of poverty from which there's minimal hope of escape."

Ken sat silent.

The priest continued: "You may have heard the quote by the Brazilian Catholic Archbishop, Dom Hélder Câmara, who said, 'When I give food to the poor, they call me a saint. When I ask why they are poor, they call me a communist.'" He added, "Now he was controversial and had various run-ins with the church, but I think he was on track with his thinking here: We need to be asking *why* people are poor, and then we must ask what we as Christians can do about it."

Braxton interrupted, "Look, Ken, we're not wanting to lay a guilt trip on you. As I said yesterday, I admire what you're doing. I do. And so does

Father here. But we're pushing you to think bigger picture and, as important, to ask what harm you might be doing with your current model of 'parachute missions.'"

"Harm?" Ken asked.

"Sure," said Braxton. "Like building dependency. Reminding people of their poverty, with a paternalism that reinforces the notion that they can't help themselves."

Gonzalez asked, "Ever heard of a book called *Toxic Charity*?"

Ken said he hadn't.

"When you get back home get a copy and read it," said the priest. "One thing I remember from the book is how a church in Mexico got painted six times during one summer by six different mission groups. Maybe the church was a favorite of some organization arranging these mission trips.

"But is that what that church needed? Of course not. Or was it more the result of a system that allows wealthy churches in the US to tell poorer congregations, 'This is what you need: we're coming to paint your church'? And so these poorer churches put up with six coats of paint in the hope that maybe, one day, one of these wealthy patrons might actually talk to them about their true needs."

He added, "The book emphasizes how important it is to establish long-term relations with the people you want to work with and do things in a true partnership *with* them, not *for* them. But building a longer-term relationship takes far more commitment than a quick in-and-out, week-long visit."

Then Gonzalez said, "Come, John, we have interrogated this poor man long enough. I know he's heard the short version of how I ended up here. I don't know if he's heard your story."

30

Braxton's and Lucy's Stories

Monday Evening

KEN, GRATEFUL FOR THE reprieve, quickly assured Braxton that he'd be most interested in what he had to say.

It didn't take Braxton long. He had majored in classics in college, "A thoroughly unmarketable but infinitely gratifying field," he said. Then he entered the Peace Corps and spent two years in the country, teaching English in an elementary school in a village not far from San Pedro. He proved to be a quick study in Spanish and was pretty fluent by the end of his two-year term, he said. So he signed up for a second term, at the same school. That's when a new teacher "caught my eye," as he put it, and they were engaged within a year. "And so I just stayed on; it was that simple." Six years after they married she died in one of the cholera epidemics that sweep the country every decade or so.

"We had had no children and that left me free to return to the United States if I wanted," he said. "But my home was now here. My parents were both deceased and I go back to Iowa every year or so to see my siblings and their families."

He had continued to teach until his retirement two years ago. Of the hundreds of students he taught over the years, virtually none made it through high school. Because San Pedro had only an elementary school, a child wanting to attend middle school and then high school needed to move to a larger town. He knew of at least half a dozen who had done so; typically, these students were sent to live with relatives for the express purpose of advancing their education. He was aware of only two of his former students who went on to university. One, he knew, was now a lawyer in San Gabriel. He had heard, but couldn't confirm, that the other graduated in business.

Braxton said, "I suppose I should be proud of them, and of course I am. It is an amazing accomplishment that these two went this far. But I remain heart-broken over the hundreds of bright, eager kids who never had a hope of finishing middle school, let alone high school or university.

"I think of the 'starfish on the beach' story, where this person's throwing back a few of the thousands of starfish that have been washed up on the shore. And someone says, 'Why are you doing that? It won't make any difference.' And the person replies, as he's tossing another back in the water, 'Well, it will to this one.'"

Ken couldn't be sure but he thought he heard Braxton's voice falter and his eyes seemed to tear up, before he added: "Those two university grads were my starfish."

⚘

Braxton said that he had inherited enough money from his parents to live comfortably, especially given his simple lifestyle and the low cost of living.

After the grilling Braxton had given him the day before and this evening, Ken felt bold enough to ask if he had any church affiliation.

"Quaker, by background. Freelancer by practice," he replied.

"We see him at Mass on a totally unpredictable schedule," said Fr. Gonzalez. "And I know in his weaker moments he's been known to show up at the evangelical church. I can't think why, except maybe for their music: John's got a remarkable singing voice, I'm told."

John shook his head in denial.

Gonzalez said, "Of course, we never hear him singing in our services. Then again, our music is pretty dismal, to be honest."

"You're right there," Braxton said.

⚘

Ken's praise for the meal led Gonzalez to tell Lucy's story. Her husband was one of the fourteen villagers killed in the civil war, nearly a quarter of a century ago. Unable to farm their smallholding on her own, with four children under the age of ten, she was forced off the property by the landowner. She was initially supported by relatives but obtained a measure of financial security when Gonzalez's predecessor had hired her as a housekeeper, which was her only source of income. She now lived in a simple house in the village.

"It's as well she's superb at what she does, especially her cooking," Gonzalez said. "If she wasn't I'd have a real problem because I wouldn't have the heart to fire her."

Gonzalez then launched into a thoughtful analysis of the supportive role that housekeepers played in the lives of Catholic priests.

"They're the unsung heroes of the church's pastoral ministry," he continued. Without wives, priests rely more than they'd like to admit on the companionship of their housekeepers, to say nothing of the running of the house: cleaning, cooking, shopping—all things that would eat significantly into a priest's time.

"And sometimes their diplomatic skills can save the day. The story's told," he said, "about the church busybody showing up at the rectory. The priest sees her coming and dashes to hide in his study, telling the housekeeper, 'Please deal with her; I just don't have the energy to face her today.'

"So the housekeeper meets Mrs. Brown at the door, invites her in and makes her a cup of tea and entertains her after coming up with a plausible explanation why the priest isn't available.

"After about an hour the priest quietly opens his study door and, hearing no more conversation, thinks it's safe to call out, 'So, has that old busybody gone?'

"Unfortunately, Mrs. Brown is still alive and well and present in the living room. But the housekeeper responds, 'Oh yes, she left ages ago; we've got Mrs. Brown with us now.'"

Braxton and Ken loved the punchline to what the priest conceded may have been an apocryphal story but one that nevertheless made his point.

Gonzalez then mentioned what he called "the dirty little secret of the downside" of housekeepers working for celibate priests. Or, as he added, "supposedly celibate priests." Their vocation was inherently lonely, he said, and some priests—and their housekeepers—took companionship a step too far.

They then moved on to another topic. Braxton left first, leaving Ken to chat with Gonzalez for another twenty minutes. He asked the priest, "Is there any particular reason John seems so hostile toward what he calls our 'parachute' approach to missions?"

Gonzalez replied, "Well, he's supportive of missions. But because he's so aware of the deep needs in this country, it annoys the hell out of him when he sees resources squandered in a well-intended way. He would far rather have seen the money you spent on painting supplies, and on room and board for your group, oh yes, and your airfares, all going to something truly needed in this community. Or the one you were planning to serve.

"What if you used that money to start the *process* of building and funding a small clinic? In other words, you don't hire one local laborer to start working until you've lined up the funds to hire staff and support the clinic for a ten-year period. Could your church commit to doing that?"

Ken said nothing.

"What would it take to hire a full-time nurse?" Gonzalez asked. "Where would she live? What about a supply of meds? Do you need a pharmacist as well? Would you have a system to get really sick people to hospital in Santa Gabriella? And a hundred other questions I've not even thought of.

"All of this would take planning, consultation with the locals and government officials. And time. You'd need to send repeated teams our way who knew what they were doing, and who would build trust over time."

Ken interjected, "What about our group then, are you saying they're wasting their time? And me too?"

"Not necessarily. There's no telling what spark may be triggered in your young people and what kind of ministry God may use them for in the years ahead. But John and I share a concern that these trips are just a terribly inefficient use of resources."

Ken was about to interrupt when Gonzalez raised his hand to stop him: "Yes, you can quote me the passage about the sheer extravagance of Mary Magdalene's anointing of Jesus; not a rational economic action. But I think that by and large God expects us to do things the best way we know how.

"If your goal is simply to expose a group of young people in what is—and forgive my cynicism here—a self-indulgent exercise that's really intended to make them feel good, then go ahead. But if you're truly seeking any meaningful change to the San Pedros of this world, you're fooling yourselves."

Ken said, "It's late. I should be going." They exchanged departing pleasantries. However, as he headed back to the home the cordial end to the evening was offset by Braxton's and Gonzalez's critiques. Like that Jesuit instructor in seminary, who forced him to think more broadly about Catholics, his two dinner companions were proving difficult to argue against.

31

Mice

Monday Evening, Late

KYRSTIE AND KYRA WERE assigned to the home of Mr. and Mrs. Moreno, an elderly couple, both hard of hearing. He was in his early seventies, she in her late sixties. As a young man he had served in the military, in an infantry unit, around loud explosives that took a toll on his hearing. He had subsequently worked in Santa Gabriella as a low-level government clerk until his retirement. He had acquired a smattering of English, which was as well because neither of the First Church girls had a word of Spanish between them. The couple struggled with the girls' names, partly because of their hearing. They called each of them Kristy.

The two Kristy's had to share a bed. The bed was large enough and they were relatively petit so it worked out OK. The room was small, though, which left little space around the bed for their possessions, some of which they could squeeze under the bed.

Last night was the first they'd spent at the Morenos' home; Saturday they had stayed with another family. The Morenos were devout Catholics and some of their furnishings left the girls somewhat unsettled. Kyrstie, in particular, was uncomfortable with the rather gory crucifix on the wall above the bed. She wondered if she would find it less intrusive if she slept with her head right under it, without having to look at it—but knowing it was hovering over her the entire night. Or should she suggest Kyra take that position? That way, her head was at the foot of the bed and she might at least have some control over making eye contact with this strange Catholic artifact. Without letting Kyra know of her discomfort, she chose to go with the head-at-the-foot-of-the-bed option rather than have the crucifix right above her head all night.

The family also had scattered around the house numerous other plaques, statuettes, and at least half a dozen crucifixes, all with bloodied hands, feet and sides. The most vivid was in the bathroom. The Morenos were one of the few families in San Pedro to have an indoor toilet and Kyrstie had to shut her eyes while sitting on the john to avoid making eye-contact with Jesus on the opposite wall.

They had slept reasonably well on Sunday night. But each of them had heard barely audible rustling noises. The girls assumed the sounds were normal, perhaps the wind rustling outside.

But the mice had discovered a half-eaten granola bar in Kyra's back-pack. Tonight they returned for more, apparently sharing their good fortune with their extended family. Tonight, clearly, was to be a rodent fiesta.

The girls dropped off to sleep quickly. However, after about an hour, Kyra, the lighter sleeper of the two, thought she heard the same kind of noise she had the night before. It was louder this time. Still, in her mind-fogged state, she dismissed it.

For reasons nobody could figure out, for who can know the minds of mice, one of them took it upon himself to explore beyond the granola bar now feeding his family. Perhaps attracted by the unfamiliar scent of the two girls, or who knows what, it made its way on to the top of the bed.

Kyra thought she felt some movement by her legs but, still groggy with sleep, attributed it to Kyrstie. But when the mouse ran across her bare arm, lying on top of the covers, she wakened instantly and fully—and screamed.

Kyrstie followed her immediately into wakefulness and with commendable speed switched on her small flashlight, which she kept under her pillow whenever she slept in unfamiliar surroundings.

The first image caught in the light was of a grim and bloody Jesus staring at her through the darkness. She screamed. Maybe it was a subconscious reaction, in response to the abundance of "wrath of God" sermons she had heard in her previous, and strongly judgmental, church.

By now, Kyra was struggling out of the covers, still screaming, and frantically brushing away at whatever living thing had invaded her space.

Kyrstie woke enough to remember where she was and who her screaming bed-partner was, although she didn't know the cause of her distress. She assumed it must have been a nightmare and tried to calm her: "It's OK, Kyra, it's OK—it's me, Kyrstie."

"It was a rat," said Kyra. "On my arm, a rat."

"It's OK, Kyra," Kyrstie repeated. "You were just having a dream, a bad dream. It's OK."

"No, I swear, there was something on my arm," she insisted. "I tell you, it was a rat. Or maybe a mouse; it was so quick, I couldn't be sure."

Kyrstie got out of bed and with the help of her flashlight shuffled her way in the narrow space between the wall and the bed to the light switch. The single, unshaded bulb came to life, revealing only the two girls and a tangle of bedding. No mouse. Or rat.

"I swear, it was moving," said Kyra.

And at that moment it did: an athletic mouse emerged from under one of the blankets and sprinted across the bedding, off the bed, onto the floor and straight through a half-inch gap under the door.

Kyrstie shrieked and leaped onto the bed, where Kyra was sitting, shaking and hugging her knees. The bed collapsed. This development sent the remaining mice in the same direction as the first one. The girls weren't intentionally counting the now-exiting intruders but later agreed in re-counting the story that there must have been at least three or four.

Mr. and Mrs. Moreno, neither of whom could afford hearing aids and wouldn't have slept with them even if they had, heard nothing.

The girls now decided that they needed to check for any remaining mice. That task fell to Kyrstie, who had the flashlight. She gingerly climbed off the bed, now lying askance on the floor, and looked for vermin. She picked up her backpack first and shook it at arms' length. Nothing exited. Then she did the same with Kyra's backpack, home of the half-eaten granola bar. Again, no sign of mice. Kyra joined Kyrstie on the floor, barely fitting into the narrow space between the bed and the wall. Using the flashlight they did a thorough scan of the space under the bed and the rest of the room.

Concluding that the only way mice could get in was under the door, they took one of the blankets, rolled it up and put it by the door, with their backpacks on top to weigh it down and prevent the mice from making an encore appearance. One blanket short on the bed meant they might be cold so they each put on another top.

Then they had to figure out the bed, which had a few minutes before succumbed to Kyrstie's terrified leap. Again, with the help of the flashlight, they concluded that the bed hadn't actually broken; the frame had simply disconnected from the headboard. Between them the girls managed to get the pieces together again.

With the space under the door secured, and the bed fixed, they switched off the light. The girls carefully climbed back on the bed, as if to test their handiwork. It held. Then, just as they were settled, Kyra realized what she'd been distracted from in the chaos and said, "Oh no, I need to pee."

Kyrstie handed the flashlight to her friend and, remembering the ever-watchful Jesus in the john, hoped her friend would be OK.

Neither of them slept well that night.

32

Ricardo Gets Busy in Santa Gabriella

Tuesday Morning

THE PREVIOUS DAY'S TRAFFIC wasn't as bad as Ricardo feared. Normally Mondays are busy days for truckers but for whatever reason the section of Highway 101 between San Gabriel and Santa Gabriella was quieter than usual. He made good time, even with a break for lunch, and checked into a hotel near the airport just after 6:15 p.m.

Driving tired him and he was also hungry. Across the road was a Burger King, where he grabbed a take-away combo meal. Then, sitting in his hotel room, by a cramped table, he got out his notebook, pen and phone, and began plotting what Tuesday morning should look like.

After a solid sleep he awoke just after 6:30 and returned to the Burger King for a breakfast combo, this time including coffee. He expected it to be mediocre but he didn't want to spend time hunting for better fare. So, back in his room, he ate while reviewing last night's notes.

With the confirmation that the group had indeed arrived in Santa Gabriella on Saturday evening, his action steps, and their results, were as follows:

- Check with Pastor Sanchez that the group hadn't somehow found their way across the mountains to his church, perhaps by taking a connecting flight yesterday. *No, they hadn't.*

- Check with Clara Small at Mission Matchers HQ to see if she had an update. *No, she didn't.*

- Contact the local police headquarters. *The sergeant he reached was suspicious and uncooperative, until Ricardo stretched the truth by saying that the missioners were a muy importante group of Americans. He implied there could be a major diplomatic incident if the national commissioner of police had to intervene if Ricardo didn't get honest answers. The sergeant then assured Ricardo they had no record of any groups of Americans having difficulty or otherwise coming to police attention over the past few days.*

- Check with the local hospital. *Another blank.*

Then he walked the 500 yards to the airport, to gather information face-to-face. He had four destinations on his list.

- Visit the local Delta representative to glean whatever new information he could. *The supervisor confirmed what was already known, that the group had arrived and, a new detail, their luggage was still unclaimed.*

- Check in person with the staff at the car rental counters at the airport, to see if a group of Americans had rented any vehicles on Saturday night. *Some companies were reluctant to share their information but Ricardo's diplomatic skills got the confirmation he expected: no, no rentals. (He knew this was a long shot but wanted to eliminate this possibility.)*

The third and fourth were to:

- Visit the taxi ranks to learn what he could, and

- Visit the airport office of ONSI, the *Oficina Nacional de Servicios de Inmigración* (the National Bureau of Immigration Services).

The taxi rank visit provided his first major breakthrough. Ricardo's main interest was to learn what options a group of eleven American missionaries might have pursued if they had not connected with their driver. The drivers were talkative souls and it didn't take Ricardo long to learn the amusing story about two drivers, Carlos and Enrique. They had each picked up a generous fare—$40 apiece—on Saturday night, some Americans who wanted to go to San Pedro.

Then the drivers participating in the conversation began laughing at this point. It turned out the two men got stuck on the other side of the bridge because of the rain. They not only had to pay to stay in a hotel but then lost at least two days of work. It served them right because no driver in his right mind would have risked being trapped the other side of the bridge.

"Maybe they will get back today," said a driver who was relishing the story, "or maybe they will send for their families and start a new life on the other side of the bridge." The other drivers laughed uproariously, with the storyteller slapping his thigh as he doubled over with laughter. Ricardo thanked the men, who greatly enjoyed finding a new audience for this story of what they saw as a fitting punishment for greed. At last, Ricardo thought, a concrete lead, and a trail toward another San Pedro.

Minutes later this was confirmed by the helpful officer staffing the airport's ONSI office. Yes, he had heard about a group of American missionaries who had arrived. The passport officer forwarded the arrival information to the regional office. Then a routine check revealed that the group didn't have the necessary permit to be in San Pedro.

"What would have happened next?" Ricardo asked.

"Oh, they would have contacted the national police," the official replied.

Ricardo was too smart to believe that everything in life was black and white. But when it came to the country's national police, his experience was that with few exceptions, they were divided into two groups: "corrupt/incompetent/unprofessional thugs," on the one hand, and "even more corrupt/incompetent/unprofessional thugs" on the other.

❧

He needed to regroup. His first impulse was to phone Carla at Mission Matchers to tell her what he had discovered. The group had indeed made their way toward another village named San Pedro. He assumed that Ken and the First Church group would have tried to connect with a church in this village. Where to look next? Going on-line with his phone to see what churches might be in this village was close to pointless, small churches in small villages would almost certainly not have a website. But there was one possible lead: The Catholic presence throughout the country might include a priest in or near this village.

Google helped him find the local bishop's office in Santa Gabriella. The person taking his call told him that yes, the priest in that area was a Fr. Gonzalez.

"And do you have a phone number for him?" Ricardo asked, sensing that he was closing in on his target.

"*Lo siento*—sorry," said the woman. "I can give you his number, but that won't help you: That whole area is off the grid when it comes to phones because they're in a dip or something. You can't reach him unless he's come to Santa Gabriella."

Ricardo took down the number anyway and thanked the woman. Then he drove to the truck stop he had noticed on his arrival in town last night. Chatting with the drivers, who knew the territory as well as anyone, Ricardo found out that the main bridge on the road to San Pedro was still flooded but that the water level was dropping fast and would likely be passable by late today.

He returned to his hotel room and phoned Carla. She agreed with his proposal to drive to San Pedro late that day and try to connect with Ken. Meanwhile, he would phone Pastor Lawrence and give him the good news that Ricardo had found the group.

Well, nearly.

33

Devotions for a New Day
Tuesday Morning

By Tuesday morning, Ken was so focused on adjusting to the group's radically new circumstances that he had more or less forgotten about Ricardo. One thing he did want to stick to, though, was his plan for a devotional each morning. Yesterday Officer Manuel had cut that short. But today he expected they would get back on track.

As arranged, the group gathered at Pastor Alfredo's church just before 9. The pastor was there too and, Ken noticed, greeted at least half the group by name. Ken was impressed.

Everyone was present, except a still-under-the-weather Annabel. Even sleep-deprived Kyra and Kyrstie made it. They went inside the church and sat in the first two rows of benches.

Ken asked how things were going. Kyra told of their eventful night and asked, "Ken, can we be moved to a different family? We really don't want to go through that again."

Ken replied, "Tell you what, let's talk afterwards, OK?" He still had to address the theft issue with Alfredo. He now had Bill's and Zach's passports, which he hoped were safer with him. Now this business with the mice . . . It would be tricky, he feared, to move the students; he would need the priest's advice on the best way to deal with the Morenos, who might be deeply hurt if their hospitality was seen as deficient.

Setting these thoughts aside, he launched into a five-minute devotional, based on Paul's Damascus Road experience in Acts 9. "We've not been blinded, fortunately," told the group. "But as with Paul the goal of our journey has certainly been turned upside down. We didn't come on this trip to do the harm to God's people that Saul wanted to do, but like him we've found that our original plans and God's plans for us didn't coincide."

Murmurs of agreement from the group followed.

"So, like Saul, whose very identity is changed by this experience and he becomes Paul, we too are still trying to find out what God wants of us. I want each of you to be thinking about this question: How is this experience, which I know isn't what we expected, making you someone who is better equipped to serve the Lord, just as Paul was?"

He said a short prayer and turned to Alfredo to learn what the day's assignments were. In fact, they were the same as Monday's.

Everyone was OK with that except Sissy. She had not had a positive experience working with Victoria Rodriguez, the stroke victim for whom she had cared yesterday. It had not gone well for Sissy. It wasn't so much because of the language barrier; Sissy had more basic Spanish than anyone else in the group. Mrs. Rodriguez spoke and understood no English. The main problem was Mrs. Rodriguez herself. Struggling with a partially paralyzed body left her intensely frustrated at the best of times. Now, compounding her frustration was this supposed helper who couldn't easily understand her slurred speech.

Mrs. Rodriguez's daughter, Alma, welcomed and then took advantage of the break; she took far longer than she needed buying supplies at the village's small store, chatting at length with Mrs. Mesa about the unexpected arrival of the Americans. Then she popped in on a friend for an extended cup of coffee.

Alma had gained the impression that Sissy was a qualified nurse and she assumed this experienced aide would take good care of her mom. Who knows? Maybe her loving care would help brighten her mom's day and help lift her out of her chronic crabbiness. In short, Alma was thrilled to have a competent, well-trained Christian care-giver looking after her mom. Through no fault of her own, Sissy was far from competent or trained in caring for recovering stroke victims—and certainly not those who spoke no English and whose slurred Spanish was virtually impossible for Sissy to understand.

That lack of communication only heightened Mrs. Rodriguez's crabbiness. She'd bark out an order for a glass of water, for example, that Sissy had no hope of understanding. Equally futile was her attempt to use gestures to convey her needs to this strange and burdensome American woman. Her right arm was largely immobilized by her stroke, so her gestures didn't get across the message she intended: that she still wanted that glass of water, you stupid woman.

Committed as she was to being as good a servant of the Lord as possible, Sissy did the best she could, with the most positive attitude she could bring to the situation. She thought of the wording in 1 Corinthians 13, in the *King James Version* on which she'd been raised, that "charity suffereth long." As her hours with Mrs. Rodriguez wore on, she empathized with the old woman's plight but simultaneously saw herself as a suffering servant. Not *the* suffering servant, of course. She realized she had little of Jesus' compassion and endurance. Yet her suffering, in Alma's absence, grew increasingly long.

Then her suffering was compounded with guilt. Should she approach Ken or Alfredo and ask for a new assignment? She reflected on how her burden was infinitesimally small compared with the suffering Jesus had undergone for her and all sinners, and her guilt deepened. Maybe there was a Bible verse that was the equivalent of "suck it up." In case there was, she decided to keep quiet about her assignment to help Alma with her mom.

Ken's voice interrupted her reverie, as he said, "OK everyone, have a good day. I'll try to come and check on you. I'll start with Tim and Zach at the school, to see how you're doing. But for now, could I please see Zach and Bill, and Pastor Alfredo."

34

A Motor-Cycle Ride Delayed
Tuesday Morning

Pastor Alfredo was embarrassed and angry to hear about the theft of the money and the Nikes. "It must have been one of the kids," he said, "and I think I know which one. I'm so sorry this has happened. Let me speak to the family."

Without telling anyone, Ken decided that if the money and Nikes were not recovered, he would reimburse the boys out of the trip's contingency fund. He reasoned that their accommodation and safety was his responsibility and their loss occurred not because of negligence on their part. He therefore had a moral duty to set them right. But he'd keep his thinking to himself until Alfredo had spoken with the boys' host mom and dad. He did not envy Alfredo that task but he was the right person to address this delicate matter, knowing both the family itself and the cultural pitfalls to avoid.

He then visited the elementary school. The village had no middle or high school. As he saw Tim and Zach in action with the kids, in separate classrooms, he was impressed with how they had uninhibitedly jumped into school activities. The principal had placed them with older kids yesterday; today's classes, with about a dozen kids in each, were with second and third graders respectively.

Ken marveled at how young children don't let something like a language barrier dim their exuberance and interaction with a high energy visitor. One could tell that the kids in both classes were thrilled to have these American teenagers as their own teaching aides. Mostly, Tim and Zach did unstructured, impromptu language lessons. Zach, especially during recess, reveled in hamming it up with the kids, giving high fives, tickling a few of the boys in mock combat (he was careful not to do so with any of the girls), and making faces that reduced the kids to hysterical laughter. How much formal learning took place yesterday and today was another question. But there was no doubt about the joy he brought into these kids' lives.

Even though Tim was by nature more subdued, he too won the hearts of the kids with whom he interacted. He was more focused on instilling at least a little formal learning. He gave a vocabulary lesson that highlighted how English can be a confusing language and that they should be patient in learning it. To show how the letters "ough" are pronounced differently, he taught them this sentence: "A rough-coated, dough-faced, thoughtful ploughman walked through the streets of Scarborough, but he fell into a slough, after which he coughed and hiccoughed." (Tim wisely chose not to confuse the class by pointing out this latter word's preferred spelling of "hiccup.")

He struggled to describe what some of the words meant, especially "dough-faced" and "slough." But they loved his demonstrations of "coughed" and "hiccoughed."

⚭

Ken kept an eye on the time, as he'd arranged to meet John Braxton at San Felipe church at 10:30. On his way there he was met by a traumatized Kristen, who had come running straight from the home where she and Kyra were babysitting the twins.

Initially, Ken feared disaster had struck the twins. But no. Gasping for breath, and struggling to stifle her tears, she conveyed the gist of her story. She was visiting the outhouse at the twins' home when, somehow, her passport slipped out of the back pocket of her jeans and fell into the world below.

"I don't know how it happened," she said. "It was just so quick. I must have been when I was pulling up my jeans." Then her embarrassment at telling her youth leader about completing her bathroom activities led to an intense blush. She knew that he knew that women and girls went to the bathroom; it just wasn't the sort of thing you spoke about to men, and certainly not to men in ministry.

"Have you, er, tried to retrieve it?" Ken asked.

"No, I mean it's just awful and gross."

Ken asked a follow-up question: "Do you have a flashlight? I mean, at the house with the twins, perhaps in your backpack?"

She didn't, so Ken said, "Look, you stay here until Mr. Braxton arrives on his motor-bike and tell him where I'm going. I'll get my flashlight at my place and I'll go to the twins' house; it's that blue one over there, isn't it?"

"Yes," said Kristen, who quite illogically thought that just having informed the group's leader about the crisis automatically meant he would solve it, such was her faith in the youth pastor on whom she'd had a crush for months. But even in her most romantic fantasies she had never imagined them being drawn to each other over a passport in an outhouse.

"Then, after you've given Mr. Braxton the message, come and find me."

"Sure." Everything she'd admired about him, besides his adorable smile and wavy brown hair, was expanding to another realm: This take-charge man was proving himself to have truly heroic qualities. How many men could you count on who would unhesitatingly volunteer to go fishing for a passport under these conditions?

"Kristen, are you OK?" Ken asked, having noticed the transformation from this sixteen-year-old's frantic disposition just a few minutes ago, to her current dreamy, even glazed way of looking at him now.

"Fine, I'm fine. Except for the passport, I mean," she said.

"It'll be OK," said, and gave her a quick encouraging hug which, had he been able to enter her dream world, he would have known was the last thing to do.

Then he headed to his house.

☙❧

Less than ten minutes later Ken was pointing his flashlight into the fetid matter below. His first step was to ensure the passport was where Kristen said it was.

Check. But locating it was the easy part in "Operation Passport Retrieval." The situation was encouraging, in that the passport appeared to be going nowhere (thank goodness, he thought, that this wasn't a septic tank set-up in which the passport had come to rest).

He could clearly see the passport floating on the top of . . . Well, he chose not to describe it to himself. He thought, "It's as well I'm in ministry and expected to meet people's needs, whatever they are, because I can't imagine a job that would pay enough to do this."

Now for part two: the retrieval itself. Kristen arrived, having explained the situation to Braxton. He followed close behind. Ken greeted him and told him that the passport was clearly visible. He pointed the flashlight into the darkness and Braxton said, "Yes, I can see it."

"Any ideas?" Ken asked. "We need something like tongs."

Then Ken asked Kristen, "With the baby-sitting stuff, with the diapers and all that, do they have gloves or something?"

Before she could answer, Braxton laughed. "You must be kidding. This is a developing country, not a daycare in Manhattan."

Again, Ken felt stupid in Braxton's presence, embarrassed yet again at his own naivete. He tried not to show it and asked Kristen again, "Might they have something in the kitchen, like tongs, that we could use. Have a look."

She returned in three or four minutes, with a disappointed expression. By this time Ken had decided that the most obvious solution was also the most practical.

He turned to Braxton and said, "Here, I'm going to lean in and get it." But first he sent Kristen into the house to get some cloths to line the wood around the hole.

When she returned, Ken said, "John, I want you to hold onto my belt, in case I pass out or something, alright? And Kristen, you keep shining the flashlight on it, you with me?"

Braxton asked, "You sure about this, Ken?"

"Yes, let's just do it."

With three of them crowding atop a space meant for only one human bottom, Ken reached into the hole.

Almost immediately he jerked himself upright. He said nothing and staggered outside, with the others close behind him.

"Ugh, the stench," Ken gasped. "I couldn't breathe."

Kristen's admiration for this man soared even higher.

"Let's try one more time," Ken said. "One big breath and we'll be quick, OK?"

The second time, with help from the flashlight, Ken reached the passport with his bare hand and gripped it firmly while trying to touch as little of its surroundings as possible.

"Now," he yelled, and with Braxton holding him by the belt, Kristen moved to the side to allow Ken to stand upright. Again, Ken stepped outside as soon as he'd regained his footing. Then he placed the passport on the ground.

"Doesn't look too bad, does it?" Ken said. "Maybe you can look for something to wipe it down. Any baby wipes? What do they use here?"

As it turned out, the family did have a generous supply of wipes, courtesy of a relative in Santa Gabriella. Kristen spent the next twenty minutes cleaning up the precious document as best she could. It still looked and smelled disgusting. But it was saved from a worse fate by the lamination that protected the key page with her photo. Braxton warned her not to remove any of the pages and fortunately a good number of blank pages were usable.

Ken found an outside tap, where he vigorously engaged with the soap and then the hand sanitizer that Kristen brought him. He washed his hands thoroughly for at least five minutes before lavishly applying the hand sanitizer. Then, when his hands were cleaned to his own satisfaction, Kristen gave him a thank-you hug, one that Ken thought lasted just a bit longer than he deserved.

She could smell how much his close encounter with the outhouse had affected his clothing and thought as she held him, "He did this, for *me*."

35

At Last, A Connection

Tuesday Morning

"Well," said Braxton. "With that little adventure behind us, are you ready for a bike ride?"

"Sure. I figure my day can only get better."

They walked back to San Felipe church, where Braxton had left his bike. Ken asked, "I forgot to ask you last night: do you have a spare helmet?"

"Helmet? You're kidding, right. Nobody here wears helmets. Or at least, only sissies. We're all too macho for helmets."

Ken couldn't tell if Braxton was serious or engaging in his trademark sarcasm. It didn't matter; the fact was, no helmets were in sight.

Braxton said, "It's a good thing we'll be on a bike, and that I'm in the front—you stink! I'd hate to be in a car with you right now."

Ken supposed that he must reek and realized he needed a shower. That would have to wait; Braxton was all set. So was Ken; his phone, passport, and key contact information were in his left front pants pocket, the one with a zipper. Now, looking back, insisting the group have clothing with pockets that zipped shut could have—no, *should* have—been specified in the trip packing list.

❧

Except for Ken's unremitting anxiety the entire ride, the trip to the bridge and beyond was uneventful. Braxton was a sensible rider who didn't take chances. He adapted well to the often-muddy road conditions; some stretches were also severely potholed, which he negotiated with skill and prudence. Before they set out, Braxton made clear that this was an exploratory trip, with no guarantee that they could cross the bridge. "We'll just have to wait until we get there," he said.

Ken couldn't resist the opportunity of responding, "Well, we'll just try crossing that bridge when we come to it."

Braxton didn't see past Ken's deadpan expression and failed to recognize the humor.

Twenty minutes after leaving San Pedro they saw the first truck coming their way. The noise from Braxton's 250 cc Yamaha eliminated any possibility of conversation. But as the truck drew near Braxton gave Ken a thumbs up. Ken knew immediately what the gesture meant and his spirits soared.

As they drew near the incongruously named Rio Grande, Ken saw it for the first time in daylight. The river wasn't that wide. But there was no mistaking how easily the bridge could be covered by water. It sat in a dip, with a steep drop as they were approaching the bridge, and an equally steep ascent on the other side. Water still flowed over the bridge, perhaps to the depth of about six inches. It was easily passable—or Ken wondered, is the word "navigable"?

Braxton yelled, "Prepare to get splashed," as he rode slowly through the rapidly flowing water.

Ten minutes later he pulled off to the side of the road and suggested Ken try to get reception on his phone. No luck. They rode for another ten minutes before Braxton pulled over again and said, "Try again, this should do it." He was right.

Ken was now excited at the prospect of connecting with Pastor Lawrence for the first time since Saturday night, when he had intended to let them know of their safe arrival—so excited that he punched in the wrong number for the pastor's cell phone. Instead of hitting the final "7" he entered "9" by mistake. That got him through to a heavily accented male voice at Ace No. 1 Dry Cleaners. He hung up and dialed again, more attentively.

This time he got through.

"Pastor, it's Ken, it's me." Even though it hadn't been four full days since they'd spoken, it felt as if it were a month. And even though he knew the group was fine, Ken knew too that the folks back home must have been intensely worried.

"We're all OK," he said. Then, quite unexpectedly and for no good reason, he burst into tears. Pastor Lawrence tried to calm and soothe him long distance and it took Ken a full two minutes to get past this moment of catharsis. Like the flooding water of the Rio Grande bridge, Ken felt as if a dam had burst and he was being washed away: by an accumulation of arriving at a wrong airport; money wasted on supplies they would never use; dashed expectations for his group; intellectual showdowns on the very nature of their mission trip; stolen money and Nikes; and rescuing passports from shitholes. Well, just one. But that was enough.

Ken recalled his insight while in the jail that he had planned this trip to be a cohesive, carefully thought through set of activities. That expectation, though, was shattered from the moment they arrived in Santa Gabriella—although he didn't quite know it then. Everything thus far about the trip, and especially his encounter with Officer Manuel, showed that circumstances, fate, or God's permissive will—not Ken—appeared to be shaping this week. If there were such a thing as a "National Day of Things Gone Wrong," it seemed they were honoring that occasion each day in San Pedro. More than once he had recalled the line from a poem by Yeats: "Things fall apart: the center cannot hold." The trip, in which Ken had invested so much, seemed dangerously close to its center no longer holding. Ironically, the poem was titled "The Second Coming." Right now, Ken wouldn't have minded one iota if Jesus returned midway through this awful week and gave him the ultimate excuse to end the trip.

"Everything is a complete fuck-up," Ken told Pastor Lawrence, mastering his sobs, and for the moment disregarding the quite extraordinary grace that the people of San Pedro had shown him and his group. Fortunately Braxton was standing far off, engrossed in a call of his own and didn't witness Ken's meltdown.

"Hey, you're all OK, that's what matters. Where are you phoning from?"

They spoke for another seven or eight minutes; Ken wanted to limit the call to conserve the battery. He still needed to phone Ricardo.

He added, "Tell the parents how sorry I am for this disaster but let them know the kids are all OK. Actually, Annabel's been sick but she's doing better. Oh, and Zach and Bill had some stuff stolen. But we're working on that."

"Ken, you couldn't have known about the airport mix-up. Don't feel bad about that," the pastor said. "Ricardo and Mission Matchers let us know what happened and Ricardo is hoping to get to San Pedro—your San Pedro, that is—later today. Be assured that the parents trust you and they know their kids are in good hands." He made a judgment call and decided not to mention Andre Borgvik's quest, wondering afterwards if it would have been better to prepare Ken for this man's possible arrival in the group's life.

"Well, thanks. But I'd better go. I need to make some other calls," Ken said. "I need to talk with Ricardo and see if we can salvage anything from what was supposed to have been our week at the other San Pedro. It may be easier for him to update you when we know what's going on. I can't call from our San Pedro; there's no connection available there."

Then he added, "One more thing: Please be sure to tell Angela I'm OK."

Pastor Lawrence was taken aback. But discretion is a trait that all good pastors either bring into the ministry or else learn to acquire quickly, and in his case it was something of a mix. So unhesitatingly he said, "Sure, I'll do that."

"Angela?" he thought, getting the first hint of a closeness between Ken and the church's part-time music director that until now he didn't know existed.

Then he said, "Remember, we're all praying for you. You take care now. Bye."

๛

Ken then phoned Ricardo, who recognized the number and answered immediately. "Ken, *mi amigo*, where are you? Are you OK?"

After some catching up and confirming that the bridge was open, they formulated a plan. Braxton gave Ken a ride to the next small town, Nuñez, about only twelve kilometers farther along, where Ricardo agreed to meet Ken at a small restaurant that Braxton suggested. They planned to talk there as long as they needed and then drive back to the group. Time permitting, Ricardo could meet the group before returning to his hotel in Santa Gabriella that evening, before dark.

Braxton made sure Ricardo completed the short drive to the Nuñez restaurant before returning to San Pedro alone. Neither Braxton nor Ken wanted the youth pastor stuck there if Ricardo didn't arrive. Without needing to say it, both men knew enough had already gone wrong with this week-long mission and the group still had four days to go.

36

Ricardo and Ken Make a Plan

Tuesday Lunchtime

KEN AND RICARDO GAVE each other a prolonged hug, the significance of which was clearly "Am I glad to see you." The continual breeze from the motor-bike ride had removed most of the odor that Ken had picked up during "Operation Passport Rescue." But Ricardo couldn't help noticing the residue. The longer their hug lasted, the more he speculated on what this American's problem might be. He let go before Ken did.

Ricardo and Braxton shook hands and chatted briefly. After Ricardo thanked Braxton for his help, Braxton rode back to San Pedro.

Then came more detailed updates than were possible on the phone. Ken and Ricardo took turns filling each other in on what had occurred since Saturday evening. Ricardo reported that the luggage was still at the Santa Gabriella airport. He added that even if he had wanted to bring it, the airline wouldn't have released it to him and in any event his pickup wasn't big enough for all of it. "We'll need to make a plan about getting it and your group reconnected," he said.

The main item on their unwritten agenda was the two-fold question: "What do we do next and where should we, or could we, do it?"

Ricardo had a rough estimate of what it would cost for the group to get a round trip ticket from Santa Gabriella to San Gabriel. It was about $175 per person. That would far exceed the contingency budget, Ricardo said. Changing their tickets to fly back from San Gabriel, on the other hand, wasn't financially viable either: they had what were essentially no-change tickets, ones so expensive to change it would not be worth doing so.

And speaking of the contingency budget, Ricardo brought Ken up to date on the approximate costs he had incurred thus far, which had eaten a substantial portion of the contingency. "I don't know if you can recover any money from your travel agent for this mistake. Regular buses are available but they make so many stops that it'd be slower than a tortoise with a limp. We could consider renting a bus to get them across the mountains and back."

"Is that worth looking into?" Ken asked, still feeling some obligation to contribute to the people at the original San Pedro. For simplicity's sake, Ken said that from now on they should refer to that village as "San Pedro 1." And the one where they ended up they'd call "San Pedro 2."

"The problem is timing," Ricardo said. "Today is Tuesday. If we could arrange a bus for tomorrow, we'll need a full day to get there. Then, we'd have Thursday with them. You're due to fly out early Sunday but because of possible delays, if we went with the bus option, I'd strongly advise you to come back here on Friday."

He continued, "Waiting until Saturday is too risky; anything can go wrong on the 300-kilometer drive. Bus breakdowns are common on the mountain passes. So where does that leave you? You could in theory commit to two days' bus travel, but that will get you only one full day in San Pedro 1," he said, following Ken's newly announced nomenclature. "Or you could try flying but that would really push you over budget and you don't know for sure you'd get anything back from your travel agent to help cover that."

Ken reflected for a moment. "That's such a pity," he said, "after we've come all this way to help them," forgetting for a moment what Ricardo had just mentioned: Ricardo had learned from Pastor Sanchez that the local men he had hired expected to finish the painting at lunchtime today (with additional implications for the contingency budget, of a day and a half's wages for four men).

Reluctantly, he agreed that it made no sense for the group to head to San Pedro 1, whatever transportation they might use. So Ricardo began planning how they should get back from San Pedro 2 to Santa Gabriella. He said he would arrange for a bus to pick them up at 9 a.m. on Saturday morning, outside the evangelical church. The driver would take them to a hotel, where Ricardo would arrange accommodation for Saturday night. Ken would have to line up taxis to the airport on Sunday morning. The hotel could help with that, Ricardo said.

Unfortunately, their planned stay at a retreat center in San Gabriel was prepaid and non-refundable; they'd end up paying twice for Saturday night accommodation.

☙❧

Ricardo refrained from saying what he thought, and what Braxton had said on Sunday morning. *"You're the ones needing help."*

Although Ken knew that at one level, at another he hadn't fully grasped his group's dependence on the goodwill, grace and hospitality of people they had supposedly come to "help," and Ricardo could tell. Whether it was in one San Pedro or another, the First Church group depended on people like him, who could speak Spanish and understood the culture; on hosts, like or the hard-of-hearing Morenos, who would without embarrassment open their simple homes to people whose own homes were unimaginably extravagant by comparison; and on churches that would year after year humor "missionary tourists" who would typically come with all the superiority accompanying financial, cultural and political dominance. To be sure, these "helpers," like the First Church group, were godly people, genuine in their faith and in their eagerness to live out the gospel message. Yet, Ricardo thought, if these people were invited to Jesus' birthday party, they would buy the kind of lavish gift *they* would like to receive, rather than asking Jesus himself what he would actually like.

So, if Ricardo had such a cynical view of the organization he worked for, Mission Matchers, and the "missionary tourism" mindset they enabled, why did he keep working for them? The answer was uncomfortable. While he wasn't into the virulent opposition against "colonialist imperialism" that he encountered during his university days, he couldn't avoid seeing paternalism wherever he looked at Mission Matchers' ministry. For it was a ministry, he conceded. Like the people in the churches they served, they earnestly believed they were advancing the gospel. If this is how churches wanted to do missions, those running Mission Matchers saw themselves as facilitators who could make that happen. They were perfectly placed to help Ken and his eager young people at First Church to undertake a project they couldn't do on their own. And yet . . .

Ricardo and his wife spoke often about his discomfort. He needed the work, though, and he was good at it. Nor had he sensed a call in the seven years he'd been doing this that God wanted him to move on to something else.

Also, for the most part the church groups were great to work with, as were his Mission Matchers colleagues. Not for a moment did he deny the need for "help" for the churches in his country. They could use all the teachers, dentists, doctors, nurses, architects, accountants—you name it—that American churches could send them. But please, please, not just for a week, he thought. Send us people who are genuinely willing to commit a meaningful amount of time to us, who can integrate at least to some degree into our communities, and who will make the effort to learn some Spanish, if they haven't already.

He thought of the great missionaries whom the West had sent out: David Livingstone, William Carey, Amy Carmichael, Hudson Taylor, Adoniram Judson, and thousands more whose names didn't make the history books but who just as heroically and faithfully served the Lord. These people plunged into the societies where God had called them, learning the language and the culture, putting down new roots. Ricardo didn't think he was being mean-spirited when he viewed today's week-long missionaries, by contrast, as conveying an attitude of, "Just passing through, thanks."

Maybe he needed to look harder than he had for an organization concerned to do gospel-shaped and long-term (or at least longer-term) ministry, in a genuine partnership with local Christians. Maybe.

37

Back to San Pedro, and Then
to Santa Gabriella

Tuesday Evening

FOR NOW, THOUGH, KEN Barker and the First Church group were Ricardo's responsibility. He and Ken had talked for ninety minutes and both were conscious of the time.

"If I've got to get you back to San Pedro and get back to my hotel tonight, we should think of going," Ricardo said.

"Sure, we can talk more in your truck."

Which they did, this time though about family, politics, sport and whatever else came up. They arrived in San Pedro just after 5. Ken directed Ricardo to the evangelical church, to see if Pastor Alfredo was there. He wasn't so they went on to San Felipe, where they found Fr. Gonzalez.

The priest cut short the introduction to Ricardo, by saying, "Sorry to interrupt, but Ken, one of your girls is quite ill. I believe her name is Annabel and she's staying with Cristina Ortega, one of the Catholic hosts. She came to see me this afternoon, quite worried because the girl's been sick since Saturday night."

He continued: "Cristina thought she was getting better but if anything she's getting worse, with typical diarrhea and vomiting symptoms. Cristina thinks she's quite listless and may be dehydrated. Do you know where her house is?"

Ken wasn't sure so Gonzalez walked him and Ricardo to the house. Cristina saw them coming and opened the door, inviting the three men in. Gonzalez and Ricardo had seen numerous Americans in similar straits. Annabel was awake but obviously in great discomfort. Ken put his hand on her shoulder and asked a redundant but still caring question: "How are you doing?"

"Not good," she said, without her customary smile.

Ricardo spoke up right away. "I think we need to get her to a hospital. She really does seem weak and dehydrated." Turning to Cristina, he asked in Spanish, "She's been like this since Saturday night, you say?" Cristina said, "Yes, on and off but this is the worst she's been."

"We can take her in my car," said Gonzalez.

"No need," said Ricardo. "I am heading back to Santa Gabriella anyway. We will take her in my truck."

⚭

Fifteen minutes later they were on their way. Ken used his best judgment in putting together some of Annabel's clothes. He hoped she'd need no more than one night in hospital but packed two changes of clothing and some PJs. He got Cristina's attention and pointed to what he had packed, to get a female perspective on its suitability. Apparently he had done well as she suggested nothing else. She handed Ricardo the chamber pot, however, for possible emergencies en route. As it turned out, Annabel was a spent force; throughout the journey she had nothing more to give.

Ricardo's pickup fortunately had room for three on its bench seat. They placed Annabel in the middle and Ken sat with his arm around her, holding her to himself so she didn't flop on top of Ricardo. In his other hand he kept the chamber pot on stand-by. Annabel drifted in and out of sleep. Worried that she was lapsing into unconsciousness, Ken would shake her gently now and again and ask how she was doing. Each time she'd wake and mutter something, usually unintelligible.

Ken was impressed with Ricardo's driving skill under duress. Their earlier drive to San Pedro was efficient and safe; now their drive in the other direction was equally safe but more determined. They made it to town in forty-five minutes and took another five or so to get to the hospital.

Ken was also impressed with the staff and the admissions process. Even though this was a small public hospital the staff were kind and appeared to be competent. The paperwork, which Ricardo helped Ken complete, asked for minimal information. No payment or credit card imprint was required.

A doctor examined Annabel within a few minutes of their arrival and ordered a saline drip. He then spoke, in Spanish only, with Ricardo. Ricardo translated after the doctor left:

- They had done the right thing in bringing her in.
- In a few hours she could have slipped into a coma.
- The drip would ensure her prompt rehydration overnight.
- They're also giving her some antibiotics.
- She will most probably be well enough to leave in the morning.
- She seems stable now and they will monitor her overnight.

Ricardo then said, "The doctor told us there's nothing more we can do here." What he didn't say was that Annabel's plight was quite common among American and European visitors, who were especially vulnerable to the region's tummy bugs. In almost all cases, though, victims had a quick recovery. While Annabel's case had lingered longer than usual, her situation wasn't especially uncommon and with the treatment she was now receiving she should recover quickly and fully.

"We should find dinner and you'll want to stay at my hotel tonight," Ricardo said. He continued: "My room has two beds. I'll let them know they have an extra guest."

Ken realized for the first time how fortunate they were with the timing. A day earlier they could not have crossed the bridge to take Annabel to the hospital. Ken also realized just how drained he felt. He hoped Ricardo wasn't in a talkative mood tonight; he wanted dinner and bed. With Ricardo feeling similarly, he got his wish. Ricardo went to the hotel parking lot to talk briefly with his wife, telling her the good news about finding the group and the story of Annabel's hospitalization.

Ken hadn't had time to bring an overnight bag for himself so he slept in his underwear. He stopped in at a drugstore on their way to the hotel and he bought a toothbrush, toothpaste and shaving gear. Within minutes after brushing his teeth and showering, he was asleep.

☙✦❧

He had a dream about Braxton, Gonzalez, Pastor Alfredo and Ricardo laughing at him as he stumbled through a devotional back at First Church. Then, behind them, he saw the students themselves, all of them weeping, including the boys; Annabel was sobbing uncontrollably. And behind them were the parents. They were furious, yelling and shaking their fists at him, while he stood powerless, struggling to speak over the combination of laughter, weeping and shouting. The parents then began pushing their way through from the back, getting closer and closer, angrier than ever. He noticed that Andre Borgvik was wielding a huge ax, the kind you saw in movies involving medieval executions, and his wife Priscilla was pushing forward with a large silver platter. All the parents were chanting, "*La cabeza, la cabeza*"—which wasn't difficult to figure out: they were after his head, John the Baptist style. (Why these First Church parents spoke Spanish was one of those details that makes sense only in our dreams.)

That's when Ken awoke, sweating and breathing heavily. It took him a moment to orient himself, before he realized where he was. For the first time since he, Ricardo and Annabel had left San Pedro he realized that he should be at Ana's house and had never told anyone that he was leaving to take Annabel to the hospital. Now, lying awake, a few miles from one of his group in hospital, he realized that not telling of his departure was a trivial matter compared with everything else. As it turned out, the village grapevine had let her know what happened.

Ken reflected on everything that had gone wrong this week. Then he remembered to pray for Annabel's healing; he hoped the doctor was right and that she'd be much recovered in the morning. Then Ken made a mental note that after checking on her in the morning, he'd phone her parents to update them while he still had access to a signal and enough minutes on his phone.

He slowly drifted back to sleep, as his physical and mental fatigue overtook him. And he had no more dreams about his group's parents wanting his head.

38

Andre's Misadventure
Tuesday Evening

ANDRE OVERSLEPT AND LEFT San Gabriel later than he planned. Highway 101 to Santa Gabriella was reasonably traffic free, except for an accident on the first of the two mountain passes; that delayed him for about an hour.

Based on his Google search, he found and booked a hotel room at *La Casa Santa Gabriella*, right on Highway 101. His priority was a place that was easy to find. It was.

He had a short nap. Then, after freshening up and phoning Priscilla to say he'd arrived safely, he set out for dinner. His hotel's restaurant didn't appeal so he thought he'd adventure forth by car. Driving into town in the semi-darkness was easy enough. He found a small shopping mall with several eating options, one of which was busy and populated with locals—always a good sign.

He understood enough of the menu to order a burrito, a Coke and flan for dessert. Well-fed at what he thought was a fair price (he was inherently suspicious that the locals would exploit anyone who was obviously an American), he paid his bill and left.

It was dark now and retracing his way to the hotel wasn't as intuitive as he expected. Soon he thought he was going around in circles. Foolishly, he'd left all his maps in his hotel room. He just needed directions to Highway 101.

The next traffic light turned red just as he got there. Fortunately, he saw someone standing on the sidewalk and after opening the window, he called out: "Do you speak English?" A woman stepped forward. Andre kept glancing at the light to see if it was still red and didn't notice her unusually seductive attire. Before he knew it, she'd got into the car with him and the light turned green. With a car immediately behind him, he had no choice but to resume driving, startled by the presence of this stranger.

At that point the vehicle behind him emitted a "meep maap/meep maap" sound, accompanied by a flashing blue and red light.

The woman, who until this point had said nothing, muttered, "*Mierda, mierda, mierda.*" Andre couldn't be sure of the meaning but given the intensity with which she spoke it was plain she wasn't happy.

Andre dutifully pulled over to the side of the road and two police officers approached the car, looking simultaneously amused and disdainful. One of them spoke rapidly with the woman; they clearly knew each other. She lit into him and he fired back, before she stomped off into the night, frustrated at having her evening's business dealings disrupted.

The police were far more interested in Andre, even more so when they looked at his license and learned he was an American.

Minutes later, despite his protestations, he was in cuffs in the back of the unmarked police car that had sprung to life when the policemen had seen unmistakable evidence of this man picking up a prostitute.

So it was that within a short space of time, two leading figures from First Church, under quite different circumstances, found themselves in a prison cell in the same foreign country. Andre's stay proved to be considerably longer than Ken's; it also proved to be more costly, in money and dignity.

The assault on his dignity continued when a boisterous drunk joined him in the cell in the Santa Gabriella prison, someone who never grasped that Andre couldn't understand a word he was saying. The drunk turned to the default method of making yourself clear to someone who appears not to understand you by speaking louder. In this case, much louder.

Andre wanted to ask the duty officer if they had a separate cell for Americans but thought better of it. Following fifteen minutes or so of dreadfully off-key songs, the man fell asleep on the floor. Andre realized he had no option but to try and get some sleep. But his mind was racing with indignation at his arrest and the obvious misunderstanding that lay behind it. Tomorrow he'd called the US Embassy and they'd sort out this nonsense.

Or so he hoped.

39

Annabel Restored

Wednesday Morning

WEDNESDAY MORNING DIDN'T BEGIN well for Annabel. Despite an excellent night of restorative sleep she awoke in a hospital bed, not knowing where she was or how she got there.

"Where am I?" She asked a passing nurse who, not understanding the girl's English, merely smiled and nodded and walked on. It was now 6:30 and the doctor who had admitted her last night was off duty.

As the nurse departed Annabel called out, "*Excuse* me . . ." Then she saw an orderly pushing a cleaning cart and she called out again: "Excuse me, where am I?" Again, she got no response, other than a look that said, "Sorry, I've no idea what you're talking about."

Slowly, it came back to this high school junior: she was on a mission trip, to San Pedro; she'd been sick. She vaguely recalled being with Ken in a car. The rest of her story was either a blur or it had never registered in the first place.

Then she saw her fellow patient. Annabel was in a ward of four beds. Only one other bed was occupied, by a heavily pregnant woman who'd been admitted several nights before for problems with her pregnancy. She was in her early twenties and fortunately for Annabel, she was awake and understood and spoke a fair amount of English. She was a high school science teacher and she sensed enough rising panic in Annabel's voice that she felt compelled to intervene: "Hello," she said. "It's OK, you are in hospital. You came in last night."

Grateful for a response, Annabel asked, "But where am I; this isn't San Pedro, is it?"

"No, we are in Santa Gabriella. This is a government hospital," said the teacher, whose presence and response greatly calmed Annabel, who was immensely relieved to be understood.

"I need the bathroom," she told her companion.

"Then ring for the nurse. See that red button just above your bed? Press that."

She did and a moment later the nurse whom she had seen before reappeared. The other woman spoke for Annabel: "*Ella necesita el baño.*"

The nurse nodded and helped Annabel out of the bed, moving the stand holding the saline drip alongside her toward the bathroom just outside the ward.

Sitting on the toilet she realized she had no idea what would happen next. She knew Ken wouldn't have abandoned her. Nor could she have expected him to have stayed by her side overnight. But, she wondered, when would she see him? What if something happened to him?

⊙❦⊙

Following a quick breakfast Ken and Ricardo returned to the hospital, much to Annabel's relief. Ken was equally relieved at how much better she was. He introduced her to Ricardo, of whom she had no memory from yesterday; she'd been so out of it.

A nurse interrupted their conversation to take Annabel's vitals, before summoning the doctor on duty. She spoke enough English to ask Annabel some basic questions and following a brief exam pronounced her fit to be discharged. She impressed on Ricardo and Ken the need for Annabel to keep drinking Gatorade or some similar electrolyte-rich beverage. Ricardo told the doctor they would buy some on the way out of town. The doctor also gave her a supply of antibiotics to continue the course begun last night.

While Annabel changed into the clothes Ken had packed, he took the doctor's discharge order to the main reception desk and readied his credit card for payment. Thinking of the emergency room visit he'd made back home last year, when he broke his wrist playing pickleball, he braced himself for a bill running to several thousand dollars. He hoped his card would cover it; he had no backup plan and about a hundred dollars US in cash, split evenly between his wallet for easy access and that perpetually sweaty money belt around his waist, for a backup.

The woman at the desk noticed the card and shook her head. Ricardo said, "It seems they only take cash." Ken had a vision of these otherwise kind and helpful people suddenly turning nasty and holding Annabel hostage until he could raise a multi-thousand-dollar ransom.

The woman said something to Ricardo, whom she'd identified as *el inteligente*, the intelligent one who clearly knew how to speak Spanish. He turned to Ken and said, "Forty-seven dollars."

Ken responded in disbelief, "What, for everything?"

"Yes, that covers everything."

After paying in US dollars but getting his change in local currency, Ken was comforted to see that he still had enough to buy the Gatorade the doctor had recommended.

"Forty-seven dollars," he thought to himself. "Who would believe it . . ."

40

Dealing with Andre

Wednesday Morning

THEY TOOK ANNABEL TO a McDonald's, where she got a take-away break-fast to eat on the ride back. While she was ordering, with Ricardo's help, Ken phoned Annabel's parents to let them know their daughter was ill but was now doing well. He got Annabel's mom and after they talked briefly, Ken beckoned Annabel over to say hello and assure her mom she was alright.

While Annabel was talking Ken went across the road to a drugstore to buy replacement or backup gifts for the students to give their hosts; most of the original gifts were in the checked luggage, which they might not be able to access before they left San Pedro 2. He bought a dozen medium-sized scented candles, in their own glass jars. They were tasteful but not so ex-pensive that they'd do significant additional damage to the contingency line in the budget. He had no sense of how much money remained, as Ricardo couldn't give him any precise figures of the extra expenses he had incurred.

They planned to stop at the airport before heading to San Pedro 2. It made sense, Ken and Ricardo agreed, to get as much luggage as they could. They estimated that they could probably take about half of the bags. Even though they'd not thought to bring the checked luggage receipts when they left San Pedro in a rush yesterday, Ricardo was confident that with Ken's ID the officials would release it.

Then his phone rang. He assumed it was Annabel's mom, calling back about something. He had told her that they'd soon be out of phone range after leaving Santa Gabriella and maybe she wanted to reach him while she could. But no, it was Andre Borgvik. It took Ken a while to make any sense of what this agitated, angry and frightened man was saying. Finally, Ken got the gist of things: Heidi's father was in the local jail after coming to town to find the group and having been arrested for soliciting a prostitute the previous night. His arrest, he insisted, was a set-up. He could not reach the US Embassy and could Ken help him?

Astonished though he was to learn that one of the group's parents was a mile or two away, he tried to accept at face value Andre's story about his arrest. He took Ricardo aside, so Annabel couldn't hear, and told him the story. Ricardo reacted phlegmatically. He had worked with enough American groups that nothing took him by surprise any more. Without expressing an opinion on the reason for Andre's detention, Ricardo agreed with Ken's decision to make a detour: They needed to head to the town's police station to try and secure Andre's release.

Ken told Annabel that they needed to make a quick stop at the local police station, "to take care of something that's come up—nothing to worry about."

The police station was easy to find. While Annabel waited in the truck eating her breakfast, Ricardo and Ken were taken to Andre's cell. Ricardo told Andre that the simplest resolution was for him to plead guilty to the equivalent of a misdemeanor charge and pay a fine of about $300. That included the court costs he would have paid had he shown up in court. Ricardo said, "This way, you can be grateful you won't appear in court because you could well have been spotted by one of the journalists who cover the courts, and whose readers love stories about Americans and prostitutes."

Andre began, with renewed indignation, "But I never . . ." Ricardo waved him into silence.

After some energetic conversation between Ricardo and the officer at the front desk, Ricardo said, "OK, we got the fine down to $225 but you'll also have to pay $170 for towing and impounding your car. That's a fixed fee; I can't talk them down on that."

Andre had minimal cash so Ken went to a grocery store next door to get the needed funds out of an ATM. Using his credit card he withdrew $400. With the ATM fee and bank charges for the cash advance, the total that Andre undertook to repay Ken back home was $447.

Upon payment, the duty officer released Andre from his cell and returned his car keys, wallet and watch. He also gave Andre a receipt, showing both payments in dollars and local currency. Always one to check details, Andre asked Ricardo, "What's this?" He pointed to the payment of the fine as $125. "That should be $225," he said.

"Don't ask," Ricardo said. "Come, let's go."

To avoid being seen by Annabel they walked to the back of the police station to retrieve the Nissan. Andre immediately noticed a sizeable dent in the rear bumper. "That wasn't there before," he said. His anger at paying the bribe now rose to new levels, as he thought of the hassles that lay ahead with Avis. Then he noticed the missing hubcaps. All four were gone. The relief he felt on being released from his cell was now almost forgotten in the light of these new indignities.

⚶

Ken had not had the opportunity to learn Andre why was in Santa Gabriella. Frankly, he didn't care. He correctly assumed it was to find his daughter. Ken didn't want this trouble-magnet anywhere near the First Church group. He couldn't imagine how embarrassed Heidi would be to know her father had come looking for her. Nor did Ken want Andre disrupting the group's activities or dynamics, all the more so because of what had happened with the group over the past few days. Ken thought some of the teens were pretty fragile and Andre was the last person to be sensitive to that reality.

So he told Andre as he was continuing the inspection of his car that Heidi and the others were all safe. Annabel had been sick, he explained, and that's why they were in town rather than at San Pedro 2.

Then he said, "Andre, I'm impressed by the efforts you've made to track us down. Really, I'm amazed. And I'm glad I was within reach so that I could help you during this terrible business." Ken still had a smidgen of doubt about Andre's proclamation of innocence but decided it was best for everyone if he fully accepted Andre's account of events. Or pretended to.

He didn't know how to tell him in a gentle, tactful way not to come to San Pedro 2, especially after all the trouble he had gone to. He turned to one of the principles he learned from his seminary course on pastoral counseling: "If you have something unwelcome to say, just say it." So he did.

"It just wouldn't work for the group if you showed up. I think it would really affect the group dynamics," Ken began. "And I think you will embarrass Heidi far more than you realize."

"Are you telling me I can't even see my own daughter?"

"Look," said Ken. "I can't stop you from coming to San Pedro but I would urge you not to. There's nothing you can do to help us there. To be honest, Andre, you'd only get in the way."

Andre had always been hesitant about Ken's leadership qualities. Now his fears were confirmed. Who was this youngster to tell him not to see his own daughter and not to make sure the group was fine? He didn't think Ken would actually lie to him if there were a problem, but he hadn't come all this way to be fobbed off. He wasn't going to be deterred; he had come to help and that, he insisted to Ken, is what he would do.

"Well, as I said, I can't stop you," Ken said. "But I need to let you know there's no accommodation available in San Pedro. We're squeezed into church member homes as it is and I don't feel free to ask anyone, in either the evangelical or the Catholic church, to put . . ."

Andre interrupted, "What do you mean 'Catholic church'? I thought you were working with an evangelical church. Heidi's not having anything to do with the Catholic church, is she?"

By now Ken's patience was depleted.

"As I said," he repeated, "I can't stop you from coming to San Pedro. But there's nowhere to stay. You'll just get in the way and, to be blunt, I just don't want you there."

Andre looked at him in disbelief.

Ken continued, "Now if you don't mind, we have other things to take care of. Goodbye."

Ricardo had tactfully said nothing as he witnessed this exchange and then walked off with Ken to his truck, leaving a simmering Andre Borgvik inspecting the Nissan Versa for further damage.

As they approached the truck, where a patient Annabel sat waiting, Ricardo said quietly to Ken, "If I were that hooker I would have charged him double."

41

Luggage Lost Again and Ricardo Says Goodbye

Wednesday Morning

MUCH DELAYED, THE THREESOME now headed to the airport. Thinking through which bags to prioritize and take first, Ken recognized that whatever he decided he'd pleasantly surprise half the group while disappointing the others.

But it was Ken who was in for both a surprise and a disappointment. The man at the Delta luggage office told Ken that following their travel agent's instructions, they had earlier this morning shipped all the bags to San Gabriel, the airport where in an ideal world they should have been delivered in the first place.

Libby Waverley, desperate to make amends for her initial bungle, compounded the problem by assuming that by now the group must have made it to San Gabriel. They would be thrilled to know that their luggage would soon be at their doorstep, so to speak. She phoned Pastor Lawrence to tell him what she'd done to mitigate the situation but had to leave a message, a message to which he could respond only after the fact.

With pride the Delta official explained, and Ricardo translated, that he had managed to find a highly efficient routing via Houston and Mexico City, thus ensuring the luggage's arrival in San Gabriel by late tomorrow afternoon.

Ken responded in seething silence, with his mouth hanging open in disbelief. The official was thrilled to get rid of those bags cluttering up his small work area and he was equally thrilled that he'd no longer be pestered by various phone calls wanting to know about this group of wayward Americans.

Ricardo said something in Spanish to the Delta official, who hadn't understood Ken's perplexed reaction. The man thought, "Why isn't this American grateful for what I've done for him?" When he realized why Ken had reacted the way he did, the Delta man shook his head, and muttered to Ricardo in Spanish, "These Americans, they can put a man on the moon but they can't organize a mission trip."

⊙╬⊚

The mood during the truck ride to San Pedro 2 was somber. Neither Ken nor Annabel said a thing. She was disappointed not to have access to some clean clothes or the small gift she planned to give Cristina. Ken, though, was furious at Libby's misguided attempt at help.

That word "help" kept coming back to him. He heard Braxton's voice mockingly talking about the help the First Church group planned to bring to the needy people of the San Pedros everywhere in the world. "You're the ones needing help," he had said, and he was right. Now Ken's group was on the receiving end of unwanted, interfering and ultimately counter-productive help from back home. Was the help his group set out to bring in some way equally counter-productive or, to use the word in the book Fr. Gonzalez had mentioned, even "toxic"?

And how much *have* we helped these people, he thought, these impromptu recipients of aid they neither sought nor expected, people who have been far more helpful to us after we stumbled unannounced into their lives in a rainstorm?

⊙╬⊚

When Ricardo thought Ken might have calmed down enough he reminded him that he needed to return soon to Santa Gabriella, to make the final arrangements for the First Church group's departure from San Pedro 2. But he also needed to return to San Gabriel first thing tomorrow, Thursday, to prepare for another American mission group, a Bible Church team of twenty coming from Wichita, Kansas. Ricardo had lined them up to build a fellowship hall for a church. They were also hosting a joint Vacation Bible School for two churches.

Ricardo added that as far as he knew they were not bringing any puppets. Ken didn't know if Ricardo was mocking him and his group and rather than finding out, he just said, "Uh huh," and left it at that.

☙❧

After they dropped Annabel and her overnight bag at Cristina's, Ricardo drove another 250 yards to Ana's house. Ricardo got out of the truck to say goodbye to Ken. He had warmed to him in the time he'd spent with him. He was unlike many of the mission trip leaders he'd met, the bombastic, culturally superior ones. He particularly disliked the ones who you could tell quietly resented the locals for not having learned to speak English. He even recalled overhearing a conversation where some students referred to local church members as "foreigners." Over the years he had organized groups, he was consistently impressed by those who made repeated trips, insisting they return to the same village, town or city they'd been to before. He had come to know some mission group leaders fairly well, following their repeated visits. What struck him about them is that they were genuinely service oriented and highly attentive to the needs of the churches with which they worked.

One US church, for example, had worked with a local rural church to install plumbing and a septic tank system serving the entire village. The project, which took six years to complete, was designed by a US ministry specializing in development projects. All the labor was provided locally. All householders who wanted to tap into the water supply paid a modest amount each month for that right. Nobody got the water for nothing. Likewise, hookups to the sewerage system also required a small monthly fee, with all the finances run by a no-nonsense local committee who didn't hesitate to bump non-paying neighbors off the grid. Now the US church was working with the church leaders on a plan to bring electricity to their community of 450. Besides sending small medical teams to the village each year, the Americans also funded travel for two or three of the church's leaders to visit their home church in Raleigh, North Carolina. Oh, and there was also a modest scholarship program the American church had set up, helping high school kids to get into university.

Now *that* was the kind of partnership that impressed Ricardo. He thought Ken was the kind of leader who might be more predisposed to this type of long-term mission commitment. Pity he was caught up in the parachute model, which was designed far more for the benefit of the missioners (he refused to call them "missionaries") than the people they came to "help." Maybe, just maybe, with the Holy Spirit's prodding, Ken might yet come to a deeper understanding of what meaningful missions could be.

❦

Ken thanked Ricardo profusely for his help; he had taken care of the First Church group under extraordinary circumstances. They shook hands and hugged briefly, and Ricardo began the drive back to Santa Gabriella. He still wondered about the odd unpleasant odor he encountered when he first met Ken, who had never got around to telling him about "Operation Passport Retrieval."

42

Ken Gets an Update

Wednesday Afternoon

KEN WENT INSIDE THE house, where Ana was busy in the kitchen. She had heard about Annabel's health crisis and in a halting way asked how she was. Ken smiled and gave a thumbs up. Then he changed his clothes and washed his face. When he emerged he wanted to be at least somewhat sociable, especially after he'd run out on Ana yesterday without letting her know he'd miss dinner.

He needn't have worried; she knew the reason he had left town in a rush; word travels fast in a small village. But to confirm that he'd eat with her tonight, she pointed to the food and him, with her raised eyebrows doing the speaking.

"*Si, si, por favor,*" he said, smiling enthusiastically. She smiled in return. Then, she suddenly remembered something: she went over to a small table and picked up a piece of paper. It was a note from Bill and Zach. "Hi Ken: Welcome back. Hope Annabel's doing better. When you get a moment could you please come to our house. We'll be there from mid-afternoon, I expect. I (that's me, Bill) am doing much better now. Thanks—Bill and Zach."

By now Ana had a cup of coffee ready for Ken and he managed (he hoped graciously) to stop her putting in any sugar. She was puzzled but by now knew there was no understanding these Americans and their tastes.

After he finished his coffee Ken went to Bill and Zach's home. They were waiting for him, and watching, and as he approached the door they came out.

"We need to talk," Bill said and kept walking. Ken could tell from their faces that something was seriously wrong.

"Is it about the money?" he asked them both.

Now about a couple of hundred yards away from the house and on the edge of the soccer field, clearly out of earshot of anyone inside, Bill said, "Sort of."

"What's happened?" Ken asked. "What about the money?'

Zach said, "We got the money back but not the Nikes. It was Mario, the son, who took everything. But that's not the real issue."

Bill said, "The dad just beat the crap out of the boy and he made us watch. He hit him maybe fifteen, twenty times on his rear end with his belt. It was absolutely brutal."

The two boys were shocked. Zach continued, "He made Mario pull his pants down, underwear and all, and lashed into him. The kid's backside was a bloody mess; I don't know what was worse—that the dad did this to punish his kid or that he made us watch it."

"We can't stay there," Bill said. "We can't look the dad or Mario in the eyes again. It's the most awful thing I've ever seen."

"Alfredo told us earlier that the family would be ashamed of having a thief in the house," Zach added. "But if we'd known this was going to happen we would never have told you about the theft."

Bill added, "Apparently the kid sold the Nikes for ten bucks to some guy from another village, Alfredo told us."

Ken had no idea what to say. Nothing in seminary prepares you for a moment like this. He had some vague sense of machismo in this country and the role of honor in the family. But this . . .

The only thing he could suggest was to buy time. He told the boys, "Look, maybe just take a walk around the village, say for an hour. Meanwhile, I'll try to get hold of either Pastor Alfredo or Fr. Gonzalez, to seek advice on how to respond. Meet me back here in an hour."

They agreed and went off. Even though Ken had gotten to know Alfredo fairly well, he now realized that he didn't know where the man lived. He headed to the rectory, hoping to find Gonzalez at home. He was lucky: the man was in and listened to Ken's story.

"Sadly," he replied, "that's part of the ugly underbelly of our little paradise here. The man is the unquestioned head of his house. What he did was normal, even expected, of the man."

Ken stared at him in disbelief.

Gonzalez continued: "And the tragedy is this is how Mario will grow up, believing that's the way you discipline your kids. The odds are good that one day he'll be just as violent with his kids. And don't think that girls are spared. You have a dad who learns his sixteen-year-old daughter had sex with the boy next door, he'll quite likely whip her just as brutally."

"What do I tell my two boys? What should they do?" Ken asked.

"Nothing," said the priest. "There's nothing they can change. For them to move to some other family will obviously be in response to this event and an insult to the dad and his dominance in his home. Bill and Zach may think it looks as if they're condoning what he did if they stay there. Assure them that's not so.

"It is similar to what we said the other night about offering to pick up the litter. They'd be telling this man we don't like your way of doing things. Coming from anyone, that constitutes an insult. Coming from two teenagers who're guests in his house, is even worse."

Ken understood what Gonzalez was saying and struggled to find an opposing argument. He couldn't. So, repugnant though he found the situation, he agreed with Gonzalez that he'd tell the boys to do nothing and continue as if nothing had happened.

"Two other thoughts. The dad made your boys watch precisely because he wanted them to see first-hand that he was taking action against a son who needed to be punished. Also, the other part of this culture's dark side is the wife beating that occurs regularly, especially by men who've staggered home from the pub and found that their dinner was cold, or the wife didn't greet them as affectionately as they wanted, or Gemini wasn't aligned with Venus, or whatever. The way many of the men talk, one would think it's written in their marriage licenses that they have a right to beat their wives."

Gonzalez added that there was no difference between Protestant men, like the one with whom Bill and Zach were staying, or the Catholics, or the agnostics. This thinking is just built into the macho culture, he said, and even men of deep faith see no inconsistency between Christ's gospel and violence against family members, he said.

Gonzalez sighed. "It's an uphill battle for people like Alfredo and me. Yes, many men are the most marvelous husbands you can imagine. But it's not easy to go against assumptions that are generations old. Alfredo, by the way, would advise you exactly as I have."

Both men sat in silence for several minutes. Then, Ken said, "I'd better go and find the boys and tell them." He left without saying goodbye. Gonzalez understood.

◦❦◦

Ken got back to the rendezvous spot half an hour early. He found some shade from a sun that was now getting ready to wrap up its day.

What kind of place was this, he thought, as he was having to radically adjust the stereotypes he was forming about San Pedro 2, shaped by the kindness of Ana and the other host families; the way Alfredo and Gonzalez were such beacons of goodness in the community; and the legacy of courage and camaraderie following the horrors of the civil war. Then there was today's beating of a sixteen-year-old, one beating among who knows how many that occurred throughout the village this month or would occur the month after they left. No national hotlines for abused spouses (or teenagers) to call, Ken thought. Nirvana this was not.

Bill and Zach didn't think so either when Ken recounted what Gonzalez had told him. "Just stick it out, guys. Only two more nights. You don't have to for one instant buy into this family's definition of 'normal.' And don't think you're condoning the dad's thuggery by being there. But moving to another home, even if we could find one for you tonight, won't change his thinking; that will take an act of God's grace."

On that note, he sent them on their way, reflecting yet again on this trip how God's grace plays out in the real world of San Pedros everywhere, as Jesus put it in the parable of the wheat and the weeds, with an inseparable mix of good and bad.

Then his spirits lifted as he began walking back to Ana's house, grateful that hers was a home reflecting God's grace at its best.

43

———

The Three-Quarter Phenomenon
Thursday Morning

By Thursday morning the three-quarter phenomenon had set in. Unlike the technical phenomenon of that name, involving the psychological effects of long-term space travel, believers in the informal phenomenon assert something quite simple: Three quarters of the way through any event or program, regardless of the length, people begin checking out mentally. If you were attending a one-day event that ran from 8 a.m. until 4 p.m., round about 2 p.m. you'd start thinking about heading home, what you'd have for supper, or what movie you might watch tonight. It won't be easy to concentrate during that last quarter of the program. It's not a matter of endurance, so if you were at a four-day conference you'd easily manage those first three days but at the end of day three you begin focusing on heading home.

On Thursday the First Church group hit that three-quarter mark. They completed day six of their eight-day adventure with diminishing concentration and energy. (Strictly speaking, their trip lasted nine days, if you counted the scheduled travel day back home. But as that's not a day in which you invest energy and effort, it doesn't really count toward that three-quarter tally.) They were all adjusting to the reality of their impending departure, with both the positive and negative implications that entailed.

Ken told the group the previous day that:

- It is impossible for them to go to San Pedro 1 and they are abandoning their project there.

- They will continue to do the good they can here in San Pedro 2.

- It is too late to conduct a full-scale VBS in San Pedro 2, and
- Their luggage is now even farther away than before.

Their spirits were partially lifted by Annabel's return. But overall a lethargy settled on the group. This mission trip was far from what they had expected. Yes, they were grateful for the kindness of people who had taken pity on them and shown extraordinary hospitality with their limited resources. Yet a sense of failure, even pointlessness, hung over their endeavor.

Ken picked up on this, beginning late Wednesday, and tried to perk them up with a devotional on Thursday morning. Based on the story of God using Samuel to identify and anoint David as Israel's future king, Ken reminded them that God uses people with all kinds of qualities for his purposes—including youths like David. "Never underestimate what God can do through you." Acknowledging that their time in San Pedro 2 was nearly at an end, he urged them to finish well and take great satisfaction in the seemingly modest things they had accomplished. He ended his reflection with a prayer from the *New Zealand Prayer Book*, one of his favorite resources: "With You nothing is wasted or incomplete."

☙

Mostly, they resumed their tasks from the first few days. Those cleaning the inside of San Felipe Church had done more than its priest expected. Now they were assigned to help tidy the church's overgrown garden but because it was raining hard, Bill, Heidi and Kyrstie joined Tim and Zach in the school.

Kristen and Kyra continued helping with the twins, much to the delight of their mom. She struggled to convey to these young girls how helpful it was to catch up on some sleep.

Annabel's malady had forced her to skip any work projects. Aware that she was still recovering, Pastor Alfredo asked her what kind of task she thought she could manage. She said she'd like to help her host mom, Cristina Ortega, who was so kind to her. Cristina had already identified some chores with which Annabel could help. They needed to be inside because of the rain. The widow said she'd welcome help with delayed spring cleaning: dusting, especially on top of cupboards that she couldn't easily reach, and giving the curtains their annual wash.

Sharon, who had also been ill, paired up with Annabel and the two of them worked under Cristina's direction with several hours of cleaning, dusting and washing.

☙❦❧

All of the day's tasks were undertaken, though, with a clear sense that their time in San Pedro was coming to an end. Ken told them that a bus would arrive at about 9 on Saturday morning to take them back to Santa Gabriella. They'd spend the night in a hotel near the airport before leaving in the morning. He tried to put a positive spin on the fact that there'd be little to do in Santa Gabriella. It had none of the history and touristy attractions of San Gabriel, which were to have been a culminating aspect of the trip. All that Santa Gabriella could offer were a fertilizer factory, agricultural supply businesses, and a variety of light industries. Ken correctly assumed that none of the town's offerings would appeal to his group of American teens. One possible exception was the gallery of the artist who had made the crucifix that so impressed Ken when he first entered San Felipe Church.

He focused instead on the opportunity they would have to do some relaxing but also journaling and reflection. "When we're settled in the hotel I'd also like us to do a group debrief and see what it is that God has taught as this week, both individually and as a group."

The students knew this was coming but as for today they were thinking more and more about heading home. Unspoken thoughts included anticipation of reconnecting with family and friends, especially a boyfriend or girlfriend. Others looked forward to a favorite treat, like the family's weekly visit to a frozen yogurt restaurant. Or simply the welcome familiarity of their own bed or mom's special beef casserole.

All in the group listened carefully to Ken's devotional. Some of them found it reassuring. But there was no escaping that Ken's word that morning had strong competition from the invisible tug of the three-quarter phenomenon. If the students varied in their ability to concentrate on Ken's message, one person missed it entirely: Sissy Simons. By prior arrangement, she was off on an adventure of her own.

44

Sissy's Good Day

Thursday Morning and Afternoon

SISSY WAS GIVEN A new assignment. She was thrilled to be switched from taking care of Mrs. Rodriguez, the stroke victim. Sissy didn't know that her patient had complained vigorously to her daughter that "this stupid nurse knew nothing." The mother secretly believed that Sissy spoke and understood fluent Spanish but out of spite pretended not to understand her.

The daughter, Alma, who still labored under the misapprehension that Sissy had special caregiver or nursing skills, reluctantly asked Pastor Alfred to place Sissy elsewhere, reluctantly because she had welcomed the break Sissy had given her. But she couldn't ignore her mother's adamant demand that this unwelcome American should go.

Instead, Sissy was assigned to help Mrs. Fernández and her small clothing exchange, which served not only the San Pedro community but another half dozen villages in the area. One of these was San Salvador, which really was large enough to justify the label of "town." It held a market each Thursday. San Salvador was twelve miles away and, with the buses running again now that the bridge was open, she planned to set up her stall there once again. After Pastor Alfredo learned that Mrs. Rodriguez was unhappy with Sissy, he thought that Mrs. Fernández might be open to having Sissy's help with market day. She was and Sissy was delighted with the idea. It entailed her being ready at 6:30 a.m., to help Mrs. Fernández load the six cases of clothing onto the bus when it stopped outside the small village store.

A porter met them at the San Salvador bus stop and got the six cases to Mrs. Fernández's pre-assigned stand in the market, one stand among 200 selling everything from live baby chicks to used shoes to spices and almost certainly pirated CDs. Sissy had just enough Spanish and Mrs. Fernández just enough English for them to communicate surprisingly well. Mrs. Fernández was an extravert who loved people, even the ones who tried to demand discounted prices way below the fair market value for the wide range of items she had on her stall.

She also had an impish sense of humor, which for some reason struck a chord with Sissy. Mrs. Fernández's personality and readiness to welcome a stranger into her world won Sissy over immediately. In this older woman's presence she found herself truly relaxed for the first time since arriving in San Pedro.

Having struggled with the task of caring for an uncommunicative and hostile stroke victim, Sissy experienced a strange sense of liberation as she worked beside Mrs. Fernández. Accepted as she was and valued for her contribution (modest though it was), Sissy found she could look beyond the spiritual baggage of the past. It was a kind of Exodus experience for her, which was difficult to understand, let alone explain to anyone. She found herself praying, "Lord, I sense you're working in my life in some weird way; please show me what you want me to learn from this."

☙❧

Sissy quickly learned the basics of operating Mrs. Fernández's clothing stand, about four yards wide and a yard deep, enough room for her to spread out most of her wares. The two women and the clothing, like all the other vendors, were sheltered from the rain by a corrugated iron roof.

At times it rained so hard that they struggled to understand each other. For the most part, though, they worked together as if they'd been partners for years. Sissy helped prospective customers, almost all of them women, to select items of interest. Some of the customers rummaged through Mrs. Fernández's offerings, which required constant tidying of the clothes.

When a customer settled on what she wanted, Sissy referred them to *la jefa*, "the boss," as Sissy jokingly called her. Mrs. Fernández would negotiate the prices, a ritual that almost always ended amicably in a deal. She'd take the money and put it in the cashbox. Later in the day she designated the cashbox duties to Sissy.

At lunchtime Mrs. Fernández went to one of the food stands and came back with an enchilada for each of them. Despite the weather, sales were going well, said Mrs. Fernández. As they were chatting Sissy saw a familiar face. John Braxton, carrying a couple of plastic bags with produce he'd bought, saw Sissy and greeted her with enthusiasm. He was wearing a waterproof jacket and indicated he'd come to the market on his motor-cycle.

He also recognized Mrs. Fernández and greeted her respectfully, with an air kiss. Then he struck up a conversation with Sissy, whose demeanor took him by surprise. Unlike the defensive, ill-at-ease woman he'd seen on a few occasions in San Pedro, she was relaxed, poised and happy. And, he thought for the first time, attractive. With her early departure this morning Sissy didn't have time to put on her makeup and, paradoxically, that omission helped rather than hurt.

The market was experiencing a lunchtime lull and no customers were perusing the clothing. On impulse, he asked Sissy, "Would you like to get a cup of coffee? There's a little coffee stand a short walk from here." He asked Mrs. Fernández in Spanish if it was OK to borrow Sissy for a short while and she said fine.

The "short while" turned into an eighty-minute conversation. Braxton's spring onions and lettuce had begun wilting in the humidity. For a moment Sissy wondered if the seed of something was germinating in this relationship. She had never had a serious romantic relationship with anyone so she wasn't sure what that looked like. In any event, the prospect of anything coming from this meeting with Braxton, a man far older than her, about whom she knew virtually nothing, and far from home, was absurd. Just enjoy this moment, she told herself, of unaccustomed attention paid to her by a charming and erudite man.

Mrs. Fernández gave Sissy a knowing smile when returned. Guilty at abandoning her for so long, Sissy apologized profusely but Mrs. Fernández assured her she had managed just fine on her own. Traffic slowed after lunch and, she reminded Sissy, hadn't she in any event been doing this alone for years?

Shortly after Sissy returned the vendors began packing up and Sissy helped to pack away the unsold clothes. But it had been a profitable day, Mrs. Fernández said, especially considering the weather, and she was grateful for Sissy's help and companionship. Then she handed Sissy an almost new leather jacket that she had set aside. She wanted Sissy to have it as a gift. The size was just right; understandably, Mrs. Fernández had a good eye for that kind of thing. How such an upscale garment made its way to this woman's small business in the obscure village of San Pedro, Sissy had no idea. But she was deeply touched at this woman's generosity. She gave her a prolonged hug of gratitude before they summoned a porter to cart the now much-lighter cases back to the bus stop for their return home.

It had, for each of these women, been a good day.

45

An Awkward Day
Friday Morning

FRIDAY WAS AN AWKWARD day for the villagers and the group. Everyone knew that the relationships built over the past week were about to end. The gifts intended for the people who should have hosted them in San Pedro 1 were even more out of reach than ever. Some of the group had taken pains selecting special gifts, like a picture calendar for next year that highlighted US National Parks, a small picture frame with a family photo, and some specialty chocolates.

Ken distributed the candles from Santa Gabriella to the group at Friday's devotional, which he had delegated to Sissy. She did what Ken thought was a highly credible job, on the calling of Peter and Andrew, in Matthew 4:18. She said one never knew how and when Jesus might intrude on your routine and call you to something you never expected.

Ken couldn't tell for sure but it sounded as if there were something different about Sissy: Her presentation seemed intensely personal, as if she were talking to herself as well as the group.

༺✢༻

Host moms did final batches of laundry, to ensure that each of the group could travel in clean clothes. Moreover, they would have a spare set in case their record of traveling misadventures led to more delays on the way home. Each of the students also had an extra set of clothing, courtesy of Mrs. Fernández and her clothing business. When it became clear on Monday that the group would not get their luggage any time soon, she arranged with Ken for the students each to get the extra clothing. Total cost: $43. He gave her $50. Sissy didn't need extras, she said, as she'd brought several changes in her American Tourister carry-on bag, which the students had noticed was larger than anyone else's and pushed the limits of the airlines' allowances.

Friday was especially difficult for Bill and Zach, who were eager to escape the icy atmosphere of the home of a bullying father, and about whom they realized they could do nothing. Bill thought how the loss of his Nikes was nothing compared with the loss experienced by Mario. If the dad's punishment was typical, and Bill thought it reasonable to assume it was, that kid had already lost so much more. He wished the boy could have the kind of loving and respectful relationship he had with his own dad.

Bill was more mature than most teens in having an accurate perspective of his parents, with their strengths and flaws. He especially admired his dad's approach to discipline. His dad grew up in a strict household and was spanked for the least offense by his father or smacked on the hand with the dreaded wooden spoon by his mother. Perhaps because of this background, Bill's dad had gone the opposite way, shunning all kinds of corporal punishment of Bill and his two siblings. Bill recalled his dad's description of living in fear of his father and how he vowed, during one beating, that he would never want that kind of fear to be visited on any children he might have.

Now, Bill asked himself, would sixteen-year-old Mario, who had in a moment of teenage rashness stolen his Nikes and some cash, transcend his background? Or was the boy doomed to inflict similar punishments on children yet to be born?

Mario's father had sensed Bill's and Zach's revulsion at being made to watch the beating. A chill replaced the cordiality that had previously prevailed in the house and the already limited communication between the boys and the family was reduced to a bare minimum. The sooner they could leave this unpleasantness behind them, the better.

46

Andre Arrives

Friday Morning

IF "AWKWARD" WAS THE defining word for Bill and Zach, it was doubly so for Heidi Borgvik with the unannounced arrival that Friday morning of her father. After Andre's release from jail on Wednesday he returned to the hotel. It was much easier to find in daylight. He showered and went to sleep, having had virtually none in the prison cell.

When he awoke in mid-afternoon, he began confronting in earnest three questions.

- How much of his unjustified arrest, and subsequent admission of guilt about picking up a prostitute, should he tell Priscilla? Even though they had what he thought was a strong marriage, would the mere mention of a prostitute sow needless doubts in Priscilla's mind? *He knew he was completely innocent of wrongdoing. Would she, could she, fully accept his account?*

- Should he drive to San Pedro to visit the group? Ken had tried hard to dissuade him and part of him felt he should respect that. On the other hand, he had invested considerable money on this quest for clarity; why not take the final step of what he had set out to do? Was there something Ken was hiding? While he had trusted Ken enough to let Heidi go on this trip, the fact was Ken had bungled things, taking the group to the wrong destination and then failing to communicate with parents like him. So, while accepting Ken's good intentions, the doubts he angrily shared at the meeting with Pastor Lawrence after

161

church on Sunday reasserted themselves. "To go, or not to go, that is the question," he mused.

- Could he in good conscience be party to the bribe that Ricardo arranged when paying the fine that morning? Things had happened so quickly that he felt he had no choice but to accept Ricardo's actions in getting him out of jail. He felt a compulsion to go back to the police station and clarify, with his receipt in hand, that he never intended to pay that extra $100 bribe. He would explain that as a Christian he could not condone what Ricardo had done and that he wanted the money back. Without any expectation of getting a bribe refunded, Andre thought that at least he should go on record as not having compromised his integrity in this matter.

৩৵৹

He never got the chance to answer question number three. After waking from his sleep he went to the hotel restaurant and ordered a late lunch. In true American style, he insisted on a glass of water, with ice, to accompany his meal. While the waitress didn't charge him for the water, he paid a severe price a few hours later. He should never have had the ice, which had one particular bacterium perfectly shaped by evolution to violently disrupt Andre's digestive system.

He had come equipped with a pack of Imodium taken from the family's medicine chest at home. Yet the maximum dose proved no match for the bacterium that asserted control over his stomach and, for the next twenty-four hours, control over his entire life as well. He knew the importance of staying hydrated and between bouts of illness he staggered to the hotel's little convenience store to buy bottles of vastly overpriced water.

Andre slept as much as he could, accepting that his plans were now disrupted in a whole new way. The rest of Wednesday was obliterated. By lunchtime on Thursday, he was at least stable. The Imodium was finally working. He was still weak but had enough clarity of mind to answer the first two questions on his list: He planned to wait until he returned home to explain to Priscilla face to face the arrest, and he decided that he should visit the group in San Pedro 2. Ken's strong reluctance kept nagging him. Was there something he didn't want Andre to see? Ken's blunt request that he stay away continued to trouble him. Was this a case of the youth pastor "who doth protest too much"? That settled it; he needed to assure himself that all was well. Assuming he felt up to it, he'd check out of the hotel and leave first thing on Friday morning.

❦

So it was that at 11:30 Andre arrived in San Pedro 2. He would have been there far sooner if each village had a sign announcing its name. As he thought he was getting closer to San Pedro 2, according to his map, he had to keep stopping and asking where he was. On one of these stops he was fortunate enough to encounter a local whose English was good enough to sustain a conversation. But Andre was insufferably demanding of the man, coming across as if he were the commander of a conquering army. As a result, to spite this boorish foreigner, the man directed Andre to the road out of town that took him due north, not the north-west option going to San Pedro. That cost Andre another thirty-five minutes before he got back on track. The fact that he repeatedly mixed up kilometers and miles on his map only complicated things further.

Then there was the donkey incident. Without warning, as he was on a particularly muddy stretch of road, a donkey suddenly walked from behind a bush onto the road. Andre braked violently. He missed the beast but slid off the road and hit a large rock, putting a sizeable dent in the right front fender. Just as bad, the car was now stuck in mud that was too deep for the Sentra's wheels to get enough traction. Fortunately, some youths nearby saw his plight and came to push him out. On seeing the driver was obviously new to these parts, and judging from his appearances was probably an American, they gestured that they'd welcome some compensation for their help. Not having a choice, Andre nodded his agreement. When they'd succeeded he reached into his wallet and found the equivalent of $5 in local currency. Only the next day did he realize that because of his unfamiliarity with this country's money he had given his helpers a bill worth $50.

On confirming he was indeed now in San Pedro 2, Andre looked for signs of an American presence. He slowly drove around the small village, drawing stares from the few locals who saw someone who was clearly out of place. As they noticed his muddy and dented Nissan, they wondered what kind of person would drive such a small vehicle in this part of the country.

He in turn was judging them and their village. When Heidi first expressed interest in going on the mission trip, he visualized San Pedro as a quaint village, with colorful houses and cheerful people grateful for the contribution of these self-sacrificing American youths. Instead, the San

Pedro he now saw was a nondescript settlement with dirt roads muddied by heavy rain and sullied with years of litter; mostly dull grey concrete block houses; and suspicious, even sullen people staring at him as he drove around. Without realizing it, Andre had expected Switzerland and what he got was San Pedro 2.

He found the village store and stopped in to enquire about the group. Somehow, he made himself understood and the storekeeper took him outside and pointed to the school. Andre began walking in that direction, careful not to slip on the muddy road.

As he approached the building he could tell that the school was not in great shape. Several windows were either cracked or broken. The front door, which was standing open, hung off center because one of the hinges was loose. Upon entering the school Andre noticed that the hideously green paint in the corridor was peeling. Several ceiling tiles were missing and wiring was hanging haphazardly on the wall, fortunately well out of reach of the children. Just inside the building was the school office, occupied by the school secretary, a sunny woman who brought some brightness to this gloomy enterprise.

"*Buenos dias,*" she said. "*Puedo ayudarle?*" While he didn't understand her meaning, her intonation was clear.

"I'm looking for the Americans."

"*Los Americanos?*" she said. "*Si, si. Uno momento, por favor.*" She then got up and disappeared into the innards of the building. About a minute later she returned. Behind her was a puzzled Zach, whom she had dragged away from a game of Simon Says, by tapping him on the shoulder and beckoning him to follow her.

"Mr. Borgvik!" he blurted out. "What are you doing here?"

"Never mind. Can you tell me where Heidi is?"

"Sure, she's in one of the classrooms, working with the kids. Do you want me to get her for you?"

"Yes," barely believing that he had succeeded in his mission. Then, remembering his manners, he added, "Please."

⊙╬⊚

After Andre reconnected with his flabbergasted daughter, who needed a few minutes to adjust to the reality of her impetuous father's arrival, he asked her how the trip was going and if she was well. Not that he was truly interested in her answers; he had already decided to take her away from

San Pedro's squalor. This wasn't a fit place for a young woman, he said. Then there were the health issues. He told her that he didn't want her to be the next Annabel, who needed hospitalization because of this unsanitary place. His own bout with a hostile bacterium was fresh in his mind. Also, hardly anyone spoke English. How could you serve people who can't even understand how you're trying to help them?

Humiliated, Heidi was furious at her father's intrusion. She was seventeen, not seven. Her parents had given permission for her to go on this trip and she saw no reason why her dad should now try to revoke it. She adamantly refused to return with him.

"Anyway," she said, "it's only one more day. We leave for Santa Gabriella tomorrow." She also explained that if she went with him either he would have to change his ticket to fly out of Santa Gabriella, or she would have to change hers to leave from San Gabriel. He hadn't thought of that but was unwilling to give ground.

By now their argument just outside the school's main entrance was drawing a crowd. Zach and the three other students had come in disbelief to see what Mr. Borgvik wanted. The school secretary was struggling to follow the argument, as were a handful of passers-by on the road.

Andre told Heidi, "Get your stuff; we're leaving."

"I want to see Ken," she responded. "He's in charge of this group, not you."

"Yes, I want to see him too—I'm telling him you're heading home, now."

At this point, Bill thought it wise to bring Ken into the picture. He knew that he was having coffee with Pastor Alfredo and Fr. Gonzalez, at the rectory, and went to call him.

Andre and Heidi observed something of a truce until Ken arrived.

◈

Ken had assumed that when Andre didn't show up on Thursday, that this annoying man had heeded his request. He had not told Heidi that her father was a short drive away. And he had certainly not told her why Andre had contacted him. Assuming that Andre had headed back home, he was therefore all the more astonished and angered when he got word that he was now in San Pedro.

He couldn't very well order him to leave. But he had this mental picture of him telling Andre, "This town isn't big enough for the two of us," leading to a shootout in San Pedro's main street as the villagers looked on in terror.

His mind went back to Sissy's devotional that morning, when she had said you never know when Jesus might intrude on your life and call you to something you never expected. He didn't equate Andre's presence with Jesus' arrival in Simon and Andrew's lives. Yet he wondered how to apply Sissy's call to deal with the unexpected. He supposed he needed to be as grace-filled as possible, modeling the behavior to the group that Jesus would expect of him.

"Good morning, Andre," he said.

"No, it's not," Andre snapped. "Tell Heidi to get her stuff. She's leaving with me. I don't want her here any longer."

Ken said, "Well, let me remind you that she's here voluntarily. She's free to leave, of course." Turning to her, knowing full well how she would respond, he said, "What do you want to do, Heidi? Your call."

"No it's not," interjected Andre. "She's my daughter and she's coming home with me."

Ken stood his ground: "Heidi, it's *your* call. What do you want to do?"

"I want to stay."

Andre was livid. His face was now flushed, his fists clenched.

The four other group members were quietly delighted to witness this battle of wills and seeing their peer winning. The locals couldn't understand the words but followed with amusement the body language of the combatants perfectly well. This was going to make a great story over dinner tonight.

Andre didn't know how to handle Heidi's unprecedented defiance. She would never have dared to behave this way at home. What kind of unhealthy hold did this youth pastor have over his daughter, and no doubt all these other impressionable youths? For now, he conceded, the battle was lost but the war was only just beginning, to be continued back at First Church.

Andre took a deep breath and told his daughter, "I will see you back home." He turned his back on her and Ken and stomped through the mud to his car, oblivious to how much muck he was accumulating on his trousers. Heidi, Ken and the rest of the audience watched as Andre once again misjudged the clutch and stalled the car. On his second attempt, the gears crunched as he tried to engage first. Then he was on his way.

Zach began applauding before Ken glared at him. Privately, Ken wanted to join him but leadership demanded otherwise.

47

Farewell Speeches

Friday Evening

ALTHOUGH IT WAS MEANT to be a surprise, Friday night's farewell party in honor of the group was an open secret. Several of the host moms decided that an appropriate send-off for the group was called for and arranged a buffet dinner in the evangelical church at 6:30. Everyone realized what was happening but maintained the pretense that none of the group knew.

The scene was similar to the pre-soccer party they recalled from Sunday. A difference was that because rain was a strong possibility, this time the tables with the food were set up in the church.

As they were at Sunday's event, once more the group was amazed at how much food this small community could prepare. Having lived with these people for a week, and seen how limited their resources were, they were all the more humbled at the community's generosity. Pastor Alfredo and Fr. Gonzalez knew that the unstinting contributions by several of the families meant they would live on reduced rations for several weeks.

The social dynamics also closely paralleled those of the earlier fiesta. Language remained an obstacle so with a few exceptions the Americans clustered together once they'd filled their plates, as did the locals. One exception was Sissy's halting conversation with Mrs. Fernández, which ended when John Braxton arrived. He and Sissy moved off to the side and chatted until the speeches began.

Gonzalez went first, speaking initially in English for a few sentences and then translating himself into Spanish. He began by saying that God moves in mysterious ways and that he alone knew the reason the group had come to the wrong San Pedro. Likewise, he alone knew what good was yet to come out of this unexpected visit.

Ken went next, with Gonzalez translating. He thanked the hosts, Alfredo and Gonzalez for "helping us to make lemonade out of lemons."

Gonzalez paused and told Ken, "That won't make much sense in translation. I'll just paraphrase that, OK?"

Ken spoke about how the community had modeled Christian grace for them. He added that the witness of the Protestants and Catholics working together had likewise modeled what it meant to be the body of Christ.

Ken found it artificial to speak sentence by sentence, waiting for the translation. The rhythm of his normal preaching and public speaking style was completely disrupted. But what he felt as awkwardness went unnoticed by his listeners.

"We leave tomorrow with a strange mix of joy and sadness in our hearts," he said. "We have been greatly blessed by this community. And it is because of that blessing we are sad to leave you."

He concluded, "*Muchas, muchas gracias.*"

He sat down to the locals' applause.

Ken was glad Braxton wasn't on the speakers' list; there was no telling what he might have said about Ken and his missionary paratroopers.

Alfredo went next. Even though his English was perfectly adequate, he spoke only in Spanish, with Gonzalez translating. His emphasis was on the nature of the world-wide church and how "no matter our differences, we all serve the same Lord." He thanked the group for their work and insisted they come back. "But next time give us more notice," he joked. He joked too about how next time they would make sure Bill and Zach played for the Protestants, not the Catholics.

Then came the unexpected high point of the evening. Ana handed Alfredo a large plastic bag. He took it and stood next to Gonzalez, who said—again in alternating English/Spanish: "In one important way you came here empty handed. All your painting supplies were in the other San Pedro and you couldn't do what you expected to. But we don't want you to leave empty handed."

He and Alfredo then began taking out of the bag a small gift for each of the group's eleven members. They were small hand-painted illustrations of biblical themes, such as a nativity scene, the Lord's supper, and Jesus' baptism. Each was unique and superbly crafted, and ideal as a Christmas tree ornament. Alfredo presented one to each of the group. Then he and Gonzalez took a final item out of the bag, an exquisitely embroidered banner showing an altar with the communion elements. Its meticulous artistry was apparent even to the least aesthetically inclined members of the First Church group. Braxton had bought these when he visited the San Salvador market on Thursday.

Gonzalez said, "This is for your church, to remember your week with God's people in San Pedro. And despite what you may think, we believe God sent you to the right San Pedro after all."

Conversation continued for another hour or so, before the students drifted off to their homes with their host families to finish their packing and get a relatively early night.

Bill and Zach did an excellent job of sustaining polite interaction with their host mom and dad, and the two daughters. Mario, the son, wasn't present.

Sissy and Braxton kept chatting and when Alfredo and a few others began the final tidying for the evening, they headed off on their own.

And Ken, unsure how the morning's arrangements would play out, said his heartfelt personal thank-you's to Alfredo and Gonzalez. Both assured him they'd be there in the morning to see them off.

Alfredo joked, "I want to make sure that anyone who helped the Catholics win leaves town."

Then it hit Ken: the week-long mission about which he'd had such apprehensions was now virtually over. And as he shook hands with each of these remarkable men, a lump out of nowhere appeared in his throat and he began walking back to the house before his emotions got the better of him.

48

Homeward Bound

Saturday Morning and Afternoon

THE BUS THAT RICARDO had lined up was cavernous: a forty-two-seater for their eleven-person group. It arrived more or less on time, at 9:12, driven by a polite but taciturn fellow who introduced himself as Yonni.

By the time the group loaded their limited luggage and all farewell hugs were completed, it was nearly 9:30. Ken discreetly checked with each student to ensure they had given the hosts their thank-you gifts. They had.

Then came Ken's departing words of thanks to the assembled locals, followed by a final handshake with Pastor Alfredo and Fr. Gonzalez. He got on the bus and counted his flock, pretending he didn't see the tears on several of the girls' faces. To his surprise, it was evident too that Tim was trying to hide his tears. One person was missing. Oh yes, Sissy. As he was about to get off the bus to find her, she came scurrying toward him. She and Braxton had moments before sealed their good-bye, discreetly out of sight behind the church, with a gentle kiss, as he whispered, "Come back."

The bus ride to Santa Gabriella was uneventful. After hearing horror stories of bus crashes on Central American roads, Ken began the journey with some anxiety. But Yonni took no chances. Ken knew Ricardo had taken care of payment for the bus but as his own thank-you he gave Yonni a $10 tip on their safe arrival at their hotel.

The group settled into their rooms. Some had showers. Others explored the hotel, locating a pool and a rudimentary gym, which they kept in mind for the afternoon's activities. Yet others took a short nap.

Ken instructed them to gather in the hotel lobby at noon sharp, for lunch. He led them across the road to what Ricardo recommended as the best authentic restaurant in town. It served lunch buffet style, so the group could pick and choose according to their tastes and go back for more of what they most enjoyed. Zach discovered the magic of flan and made three return trips to the dessert table.

Midway through the meal Ken interrupted the chatter and made a few brief comments. He praised them for their readiness to flex under sometimes difficult conditions. He cited the extreme awkwardness that Bill and Zach had faced with the beating of young Mario. He empathized with Annabel and her prolonged sickness and thanked the group for praying for her recovery.

He apologized to Kyra and Kyrstie for never getting back to them about their mice problem. (They had managed just fine, using the rolled-up-blanket technique on their remaining nights with the Morenos.) And he thanked Sissy for her readiness to serve as chaperone in Irma Watson's absence. Not that she had to do much chaperoning but it was her presence that counted. He made no mention of a certain friendship that appeared to be taking root. Nor did he think it necessary to refer to the unexpected appearance by Andre Borgvik on Friday morning. Heidi had suffered enough embarrassment on that front.

Then he commended them for never having complained once, about anything. At least, not in his hearing. He told them to use the afternoon however they pleased: taking a nap, working out in the gym, or relaxing by the pool. "Be sure though to build into your afternoon at least an hour to catch up on your journaling." He reminded them of the "Describe-analyze-Evaluate" handout he'd given them before the trip began:

- Describe, or "What do you see?" Begin by describing as fully as you can your surroundings or what you notice. What are people wearing? How do they interact? What are their homes like? Who is in charge here?

- Then analyze, or "What does it mean?" Note what you're observing, by asking without judgments, "why" and "how." Why are things the way they are? Why do people act the way they do? What are the underlying causes?

- Finally, evaluate, or "How does this make you feel?" Only now should you talk about "good" and "bad," "fortunate" or "unfortunate," "just" or "unjust."

Perhaps this was a bit heady for these high schoolers but Ken intended to push them to think about what this week meant for them, as well as record in some detail their experience.

He had extra copies of the handouts for those who needed them. Several in the group had left them in their still-inaccessible checked luggage.

"You're on your own till 6, when we'll gather in the lobby for dinner," he said. "Please don't leave the hotel. Remember, we're not in a small, safe village now."

Bill and Zach immediately thought how young Mario wouldn't agree with Ken's description of San Pedro as "safe."

Ken told the group about the small art gallery containing the work by the artist who had made the crucifix in San Felipe Church, which had so impressed him. He asked if there were anyone interested in joining him in what he estimated was a fifteen-minute walk, based on the directions Gonzalez had given him. Nobody was.

They finished their lunch and returned for an afternoon of comparative freedom, the first unregimented time they'd had since leaving home a week earlier.

Ken decided to skip a visit to the art gallery; he wasn't even sure it was open on a Saturday afternoon. He returned to his room. He and Sissy each had singles; the students were sharing. Alone at last, he checked his phone. Both the battery life and number of remaining minutes were good. He dialed and got through to Angela.

49

Debriefing—Part 1
Saturday Evening

KEN DIDN'T WANT TO venture far afield for dinner and based on the positive reviews from the students about lunch, they returned to the restaurant across the road. Dinner was a la carte and Ken set a maximum amount each person could order off the menu and the restaurant once again satisfied the eleven Americans.

After dinner they gathered in a lobby area, just off the main check-in area at the hotel. While not a formal meeting room, the space was relatively private. Ken had asked the front desk if they could keep the space available for them and the clerk on duty was glad to oblige.

"Well, it's been quite a week," Ken began. "Now, as we look back, the question is what have you learned? About yourself, about the people we met, about God? And about missions."

The ensuing discussion was, by design, unstructured and gave the group freedom to touch on various topics. They spent much time discussing how language proved to be even more of a barrier than they anticipated—the "ongoing legacy of the tower of Babel," as Ken put it.

Annabel said how she had a mixed blessing in communicating with Cristina; she felt they had established a rich relationship in a short time but thought it could have gone much deeper if they could have spoken each other's language.

Sissy, whose Spanish was the strongest in the group, agreed. She said that even though she and Mrs. Fernández communicated well enough, she wished she'd been better prepared. She then shared an insight she had while looking after Victoria Rodriguez, the stroke victim. That had been difficult for her, she admitted. "Part of the problem was that this woman was physically unable to speak properly. Imagine if you'd had a stroke that completely deprived you of speech. Your mind is still functioning; you know what you want to say. But nothing comes out."

She continued: "People who don't know your situation may think you're stupid or have nothing to communicate. But if you don't have a common language, the fact is that both of you are rendered mute."

Paradoxically, Zach said that following the incident of Mario's beating, he was glad they weren't able to speak much to their host mom and especially host dad. "Our limitation served as a kind of protective shield," he said. "If we'd been with English speakers, we may have felt compelled to have a really tricky conversation with them. Yeah, we were shocked at what we saw," he continued. "Maybe it was cowardice on our part but I was glad I had the excuse of not being able to express my feelings to the dad. So we all just pretended in silence that nothing had happened."

Then they shifted into a discussion of poverty. Bill spoke up about his $150 Nikes and how he had never thought how tempting they'd be to a kid like Mario—and how Mario didn't have a clue of their real value by selling them for a mere $10.

Sharon said, "I was expecting the people we'd meet to be poor. You know, with little money. But now I think poverty is bigger than just money. It seems almost everyone we met just thinks only about life in the village or in the immediate area." She continued, "Their world seems so small. Most of us are looking at colleges, in different parts of the country. Some of us plan to travel or already have. Our resources, or our families' resources, allow us to think bigger. So our world is bigger, right?"

Kyrstie jumped in: "Yes, when I was in the school for a few hours I saw this second-grader who had something wrong with her. Her one eye was all cloudy and messed up. Maybe she was even blind in that eye; I don't know.

"I wondered if this could have been treated so I asked the teacher what was wrong with the girl and she said she didn't know. She told me the mom had taken the girl to a clinic in Santa Gabriella a couple of years ago and they said she should go the capital and see an eye specialist."

Kyrstie shook her head and said, "It was so sad: the teacher just shrugged and said, 'I guess the mom didn't do anything about it.' Just think if that was one of us: our parents would have done anything to get us looked at. But this woman just accepted this was how things are.

"Maybe it was because she couldn't afford the bus fare to the eye clinic in the capital city. Or would have had to pay to stay in a hotel or something." But Kyrstie thought it was part of a bigger picture: The mom's horizons were so limited that she didn't think anything else could be done.

"I never met the girl's mom," she said. "But I'm sure she loves her daughter just as much as our parents love us. Yet her worldview didn't allow her to think about a bigger picture. Maybe you could call it a poverty of world view."

Others chipped in about the tangible costs of poverty, besides limited health care (or, more accurately, non-existent health care) in the village. Same with schooling. Ken cited the dropout rates he'd learned from Braxton. The group readily grasped the cyclical nature of poor education and poor health and low incomes becoming self-perpetuating limits on what the community could aspire to.

Occasionally someone broke out of this cycle, Tim said. Some families had adult sons and daughters now living in larger centers and were doing relatively well financially. Those that helped their families back home, with the limited amounts of cash they could send them, were only putting band aids on the poverty in which their parents remained trapped.

Ken thought again of what he had learned from Braxton and Fr. Gonzalez, about how churches and Christian relief organizations were good at emergency help: sending in the food parcels, tents, blankets, medical supplies, and so on during a crisis. Yet they were, generally speaking, uninterested in the long-term development needed to break the cycle of poverty.

Without even touching on the problems of tenant farming and land ownership by a few wealthy individuals, the group grasped the problem well enough that nobody said naïve things about how happy the villagers were. It was clear to everyone in the group that life was hard for these people, extremely hard.

Yes, back home life could be hard too, in different ways. But Ken knew if the students were forced to choose between the life they knew and living in San Pedro (setting aside language issues), they wouldn't hesitate to live where they did. The poverty they had seen first-hand, and its implications, was a lesson they could not easily have learned in Sunday School classes at First Church. That, surely, was a benefit of this trip, even if it were to the wrong San Pedro.

Ken sensed a certain level of guilt in the group and felt compelled to address it. "I suspect some of you feel guilty about what you have back home—tangible things, like indoor plumbing or perhaps a bedroom to yourself; opportunities, like the prospect of college and a decent job; and a view of the world that's not limited by poverty, like the mom of the girl with the eye problem. You've got so much that these people don't have."

He saw a few heads look down; he had struck a chord.

"I want to say two things about that," he said. "First, not one of you is responsible for the economic conditions you saw in San Pedro 2. Nothing, from the poor condition of the soccer field to such limited cash that a young boy would steal Bill's Nikes and sell them for ten bucks—none of these conditions is your fault. Let me say that again: none of these conditions, the cramped houses, lack of education and health care, *none* of that is your fault. Do not feel guilty about that.

"Then, second, about the good things you have back home. Don't feel guilty about living in a home that's built well enough that you won't have a problem with mice." Kyra and Kyrstie smiled. "Or that you have access to good health care or education. Don't you think God wants you to live in a house free of mice, and be healthy and educated to your full potential?"

He paused. He could see his message was hitting home. "Or think of the horror these people went through during their civil war: Should you feel guilty because they didn't live in safety the way you do? Of course God wants people to live in safety. And to experience justice.

"Look, there's plenty wrong in our society. But we need to accept with gratitude, not guilt, the blessings God gives us. In general, he gives us what we need to live out our lives for him. But be careful not to take more than we're entitled to. Remember what Jesus said in Luke's gospel, that much more is expected from those of us who've been given much."

Then he told the story he'd heard in seminary of a Christian businessman who'd done extremely well. He was showing his pastor around his palatial eight-bedroom home by the lake. The walls were decorated with high-end pieces of art, valued at well over half a million dollars. And in the three-car garage were cars each costing more than $75,000. The businessman told the pastor, "We're so blessed; God has given us so much." The pastor responded, "And how much did you need to keep?"

"Bottom line," said Ken, "don't feel guilty about the good things God has given you. Be prepared, though, as you get older and I hope wealthier, to answer that pastor if he ever visits you."

50

Debriefing—Part 2

Saturday Evening

THE DISCUSSION THEN MOVED to the catalog of things that had gone wrong, beginning with Libby Waverley's error in sending them to the wrong airport.

"You know," said Tim, "when you stand back and look at it, it's actually quite funny. We came here with these ideas of how we were going to help people by painting their church and doing the VBS and everything. And then we never even met them and we were the ones who needed help!"

Ken didn't say anything but thought of the related irony of how the painting in San Pedro 1 was completed without their help, more efficiently, and in a way that brought some modest income to a few local families. Ken also knew that the extra food that the good people in San Pedro 1 had prepared was not wasted. Ricardo told him he arranged to get it to an orphanage in San Gabriel. What wasn't consumed right away was frozen for future use. He hadn't yet told the group and he did so. None of them had even thought until now about the catering that the women in San Pedro 1 did in anticipation of their arrival.

⚬❦⚬

Ken asked the group, "Based on what you've experienced this week, would you say it's more blessed to give than to receive?" He paused for a moment and added, "Or is it the other way around?"

Tim spoke up again. "I think we certainly received more than we gave." Others nodded their agreement. "Come to think of it, we really didn't give them much of anything. Except perhaps the school kids. But that felt more like we were some celebrities who'd come to town for a quick visit. I don't know what lasting impact we could have had."

Without Ken needing to spell it out to them, the group was realizing the inherent weakness of the parachute model of missions they had practiced this past week. Looking back on how he and Irma had prepared this trip, and the assumptions that underlay their thinking, Ken was embarrassed, ashamed even. He had simply done what countless other churches had done, with noble intent. His interest in mission was longstanding. Ever since high school he had admired those missionaries who brought a word "from the front" during a minute for mission at his church. Then, in seminary, his theological underpinnings of the need for mission work were clarified and strengthened.

He agreed completely with whoever had said that if you're a Christian, remember that it's because somewhere in your past a missionary brought the gospel your way—or to your parents, or their parents, or someone more distant in your family tree. He had never doubted the need for the church to engage in mission. He had never questioned the *why* of mission. This week, though, was forcing him to rethink the *how*.

The closer he looked at the "how," he wondered if their trip could be labeled a failure. They had done nothing by way of evangelism; that was supposed to be embedded in the VBS. Nor were they equipped, because of the language, to engage in anything resembling evangelism with the adults. Perhaps all they could bring was a ministry of presence: helping a mom with three-month-old twins; some relief for an aged stroke victim (although that didn't work out well); or gamely joining in a soccer match in an admirable display of Christian brotherhood.

Was that it? Not much when you thought of the cost and the time they had invested. He didn't even want to think about how much the trip was over budget. Then he recalled the words he had shared with them during Thursday's devotional, from the *New Zealand Prayer Book*: "With You nothing is wasted or incomplete."

He looked over the group and silently added a prayer of his own, that each of these kids, and Sissy, would get something enduring out of the past week. As for himself, if all he had learned was to be open to doing things differently, then this shambolic week wasn't entirely wasted.

Or was it?

51

Shaking the Glory Out

One Week Later

A WEEK LATER, KEN had regained his equilibrium—at least, on the surface. He'd taken care of the mail, caught up with sleep, retrieved the group's luggage from its travels, and completed his accounting for the church treasurer as best he could. He and Pastor Lawrence set a meeting to discuss ways of handling the financial shortfall. But they awaited final figures from Ricardo and Mission Matchers to learn how much over budget they were.

But these were the trappings of things. Ken was still struggling to understand what the fragmented week in San Pedro 2 had accomplished. He'd spoken to Angela over a catch-up dinner about his ambivalence: the recurring theme that with God nothing is wasted or incomplete, versus the reality of a week that accomplished none of their original goals. Success or failure? Or was the issue how to define "success" or "failure"?

Angela was sympathetic but struggled to grasp the depth of Ken's growing turmoil. She had not heard first-hand the compelling arguments of Braxton and Fr. Gonzalez about parachute missions. She had not been on the bus as he waved goodbye to their hosts, knowing the group had made minimal, if any, impact on these people who so wonderfully modeled Christian grace and hospitality.

Nor could he expect Pastor Lawrence to help him sort through his anguish. For one thing, the pastor had no international travel experience. Godly man though he was, his cross-cultural experiences consisted of little more than visiting San Francisco's China Town on vacation or eating at a

Greek restaurant. For another, he was Ken's boss. Ken was highly averse to baring his confused heart to someone who genuinely saw the San Pedro venture as a triumph. The morning after their return he recognized the group in church as if they were conquering heroes rather than victims of a travel agent's mistake. He specifically praised Ken for "his remarkable leadership under extraordinary circumstances."

But Ken knew better and he had enough integrity not to see himself as a hero. Rather, one could paint him as the baddy in the drama, as someone who had unthinkingly embraced an approach to short-term missions that was, according to Braxton and Gonzalez, actually toxic in the long run. Admittedly, one could argue that whatever harm they may have done was minimal, precisely because their arrival in San Pedro 2 was unplanned and they didn't get the chance to unleash on this village everything they had lined up for San Pedro 1. The bags of clothing hadn't arrived and so they hadn't flooded the market for Mrs. Fernández. In other words, by sheer chance, they had more or less followed the medical rule of "do no harm." Maybe they were innocents who through pure good fortune avoided doing the damage they could have. Still, Ken couldn't shake the feeling that he had failed the group; it was his fault, he believed, that they didn't get the mission experience for which they had signed up and paid.

☙❧

Ken's mind and spirit remained unsettled. Compounding the pressure was the deadline to complete his report to the church's council, due in three days. The clarity he needed to do justice to that document still eluded him.

Now, he realized, he needed a third party with whom to talk this out. His former seminary professor, Smitty, now the late Professor Augustus Randolph Smith, would have been ideal. Then he thought of his college mentor, Karl Michaels, who was still working in campus ministry in Michigan. He emailed him and asked if they could set a Zoom appointment. He could and he did: Thursday afternoon, at 3.

After some catching up Ken outlined in detail the week in San Pedro 2. Then he elaborated on what he'd told Karl in his email: "I just can't get past my guilt over taking our group to the wrong place, even though I come up with one rationalization after another. And what's even a bigger deal is that if we'd gone to San Pedro 1, I might now be feeling even *more* guilty—knowing what I'm now coming to believe about the weaknesses of what we were trying to do.

"Then, on the other hand, there's my view of God's sovereignty, and that he can take our mistakes, even our blunders, and make good things come out of them. I believe that in my head but my heart is struggling to catch up with that idea."

Karl said, "Is the problem with your theology or your faith? I once read of a seminary professor who told his students to be wary of any theology that does not hold up 'in the emergency rooms of life.' Sounds like you're in one of those emergency room moments right now."

Ken agreed.

Karl continued, "So a check on your theology is a good starting point. Based on what you've said, I don't think that's the source of your malady. You've just said that you think God can override our mistakes, even big ones like going to the wrong mission field, right? Let's say you ended up in San Pedro 2 because of your disobedience, and that you were 'doing a Jonah' and defying God and refusing to go to your equivalent of Ninevah. Even then God shaped events so that Jonah ended up doing what God wanted in the first place.

"But in your case, it was a mistake, not disobedience, that led you to San Pedro 2—and a mistake not of your making."

Ken told Karl that someone more fluent in Spanish would have caught the difference early on between San Gabriel and Santa Gabriella. Anyone with even a basic knowledge of the importance of gender in Spanish nouns would have said, "Uh oh, what's going on here?"

Karl laughed. "Ken, it seems you're trying your darndest to find reasons to blame yourself. Any rational person would say that was the travel agent's fault, not yours. And any *spiritual* person would say that you acted in faith in planning this trip. Even when it went wrong, you still sought to honor God as best you could.

"Another thing. Where would your thinking be today if you *had* gone to San Pedro 1 as planned. Your group would have painted the church, brought forth the puppets, and probably come back with a glow of self-satisfaction, saying, 'mission accomplished' or something like that. What learning, growth or stretching would San Pedro 1 have provided?"

Ken conceded the point. "The kids in particular were stretched by having to adjust to our unexpected venue, and so was I." He chuckled and added, "And I guess that's why we're talking right now."

"Exactly," said Karl. "Ever heard what the poet Edwin Markham said: 'Defeat may serve as well as victory to shake the soul and let the glory out'?

Now, I'm not saying San Pedro 2 was a defeat or a failure, even though you seem to see it that way. But I think that going to the wrong village meant God has shaken out more of his glory in your life by forcing you to think about what this trip meant."

Karl then said Ken should reframe his thinking. He suggested that Ken should stop seeing the San Pedro 2 experience in terms of "success or failure," and wringing his hands over a mistake that wasn't his fault. Instead, what if he framed this as an occasion for identifying what God wanted him to learn and how God wanted him to grow from this episode?

"You're now thinking differently about how you would do a mission trip in future, right?"

Again, Ken agreed.

"So, see the San Pedro experience as a catalyst for your thinking, not as a catastrophe for you and the group. Firstly, it wasn't a catastrophe. The fact that these kids, and you as well, learned more about being helped than doing the helping counts for plenty, right?"

Then, without waiting for Ken to agree, he continued: "And there's also what you've said about God's ability to bring good out of any circumstances. Admit it, Ken, much of the time those of us in ministry don't really know what we're doing; we try to be faithful to our calling. But often we're in circumstances that are over our heads; we repeatedly get stuff wrong. And yet, out of our stumbling, God works out his purposes and even brings dead bones to life. What's done for Jesus is never wasted."

Karl then urged Ken to focus on whatever mission trips he might lead in future, whether at First Church or elsewhere. "Don't get hung up on 'if only'—you can't go back and change what happened. Use this experience to 'shake the glory out.' And if God calls you to a 'next time,' to lead another trip, think how much better positioned you'll be."

"'Shake the glory out,' you say," said Ken. Then he said silently to himself, "Let's see what else falls out with it."

52

A Proposal

Two Weeks Later

TWO WEEKS LATER, AND three after the group's return from San Pedro 2, Ken met with the twelve members of the First Church council, the church's governing group, together with Pastor Lawrence. He didn't normally attend the council meetings but was there tonight to report on the mission project.

Ten days after getting back he submitted his report to the council. In the course of thirteen pages he outlined the motivation behind the trip; its objectives and planning; how things played out; lessons learned; and a recommendation for moving ahead.

Under lessons learned he listed the need for at least some members of the group to be more familiar with the language of the area they would visit. In addition, he recommended that each participant be required to take out travel insurance. Then, he argued for a larger contingency line in the budget; the various unforeseen problems they encountered pushed them another $1,100 into the red. That figure, combined with the deficit with which they began the trip, led to a request to the council to provide $3,300 to cover all the costs. Jerry Binder never did come through with the gift he had promised. (Shortly after the mission group returned, Jerry moved to take a job in Kansas City, Kansas, as a regional sales representative for a national carpeting manufacturer. The new church he and Abigail joined there soon learned of his overpromising/under-delivering ways for themselves.)

A final major lesson was what Ken described as the "limited effectiveness" of the mission model they had followed. That lesson led to the action item in his report: a recommendation that First Church commit to rethinking completely its approach to missions. Ken recommended that the church abandon the parachute approach and focus on building a long-term relationship with the evangelical and Catholic churches in San Pedro 2.

The council members read Ken's report and recommendations before the meeting. That became plain when Pastor Lawrence asked for responses and comments on what Ken had written, especially his recommendation.

Joachim Estes was first. He began by thanking Ken for his initiative in planning this international trip, something that was "a most welcome first in the history of our church." Then he commended him for his leadership on the ground, first in their unexpected destination of Santa Gabriella, and then in the equally unexpected host community of San Pedro 2. (Ken decided to formalize the "San Pedro 1" and "San Pedro 2" nomenclature in his report and the council members used those terms too.)

Then Joachim commented on the recommendation. "I strongly support what Ken is proposing here. Based on what he's written, and what I've learned from Zach, I'm convinced that it makes much more sense to commit to a long-term relationship with these two churches."

He continued: "We've planted some seeds in a community that treated our people so well, with few resources of their own. Next time we do this—and I hope Ken is willing to lead another group next year—we won't have to start afresh with relationship building. Let's think long term, about what we might be able to accomplish with the people of San Pedro 2 over, say, the next five years.

"I recommend that in addition to what Ken has written, that we include in our next visit a needs assessment and an inventory of the community's strengths. How would they like us to contribute to their needs and what could they bring to the party?"

Ken couldn't have hoped for a stronger advocate or a more articulate call for what he envisaged. Indeed, it went even further than he had suggested, with the needs assessment and "strengths inventory."

But that's when the objections began. Harry Hiscock, the resident nay-sayer on the council, said, "I don't see how we're in any position to make this kind of commitment, financially or philosophically. Ken's with us tonight asking for $3,300 to bail out a program that to all intents and purposes—and I mean no disrespect to Ken—was pretty much a failure."

Ken bristled.

Harry continued. He saw this initial venture as a shaky foundation on which to build anything for the long term. Moreover, he said, "We don't have the expertise to build a program like the one Ken envisages." The overwhelming majority of churches he knew, he said, adopted the "one-week" model.

Looking at Ken, he asked: "Are you telling me they're all wrong?"

Before Ken could answer, Annabel's mom, Natasha Burger, spoke up. "What about the investment we're making in our young people? I mean, our young people are the church of tomorrow." Natasha spoke in platitudes and clichés. "This trip was wonderful for Annabel. Yes, she was as sick as a dog but when the rubber hit the road, so to speak, her host mom was marvelous. When Annabel was at her worst, this angel of mercy took great care of her. Annabel can't stop speaking about this wonderful woman."

Ken wondered what kind of argument Natasha was making: was she for or against the proposed new approach? Or was she just engaging in the stream of consciousness thinking for which she was notorious?

Natasha revealed her hand as she continued to open her cache of clichés: "I think we should move ahead with Ken's proposal. I think we should leave no stone unturned in going after this new approach. Annabel would love to return to the scene of the crime, so to speak. And I think we should be repaying the kindness of this community, which they showed Annabel and the others, of course. One good turn deserves another, you know."

Ken was grateful to have Natasha's support. He just wished it wasn't so jumbled and not so focused on Annabel's experience.

She provided an opening that Harry couldn't resist: "Natasha, I'm glad Annabel had such a good experience, apart from her being sick and all. But as I understand it, three of the kids got sick. And so did Andre Borgvik, who at his own expense went looking for Heidi and the other kids because we didn't know where the hell they were—excuse me pastor—but nobody knew, did they?"

Ken said, "Nobody asked him to do that."

"But he did, didn't he?" said Harry. "And he also got incredibly sick. Laid up for a full day, he told me."

Joachim asked, "Harry, what exactly is your point?"

Harry responded with the testiness that often accompanies a reply to this question, which implies you've drifted off topic or aren't making sense.

"My point, *Joachim*," he responded, "is that this wasn't exactly the healthiest place on the planet for our people. *That's* my point."

Natasha spoke up again. "But that woman was so kind to Annabel..." She let her sentence trail off as she wasn't entirely clear herself what point she wanted to make.

Next came Lottie Vanderweil, whose arch-conservative view of life qualified her as a card-carrying bigot: "Frankly, I don't see why we should be investing great gobs of money to help those people, when we have all these needy people right here on our doorstep. Why just this week I learned that Lacey Derwent got laid off from her job at the packing plant and the very next day—the *very next day*—they gave the job to some illegal."

Everyone else in the room knew that Lacey Derwent was one of the laziest, most unreliable people you're ever likely to encounter. Even the more conservative council members knew too that Lottie's account of events was almost certainly skewed and incomplete. And off topic, Pastor Lawrence thought to himself.

Striving to maintain an even hand, he said: "Um, let's get back to Ken's proposal, shall we. What other thoughts do we have?"

For the first time that evening, Arnie Anderson spoke up. He conceded that the trip hadn't gone according to plan and that there were weaknesses in the parachute model. However, he said, "just exposing these kids to God's wider world, in the spirit of service, will pay dividends we cannot calculate. Who knows how many of these kids will deepen their hearts for mission in the years ahead?"

He continued, "Lest we forget, God created the world, the universe, in just six days. Who is to say what he accomplished in the lives of our young people in that time? Or in the lives of the people they ministered to?" He paused. Then resumed his argument: "Do we have so little faith that we think God could not work through a six-day or one-week mission program? For that matter, he could work wonders if it were only a five-day mission trip. Or four, or three. Jesus, remember, was raised from the dead after three days." He was rambling now.

Pastor Lawrence tried reining him in: "So you're saying, Arnie, that you're in favor of us continuing these short trips, right?"

Arnie said, "Right. And another thing. So what if the trip cost more than we budgeted? What is that against a possible life-changing encounter that these kids may have had. Remember, God owns the cattle on a thousand hills. And what is the alternative? If we conclude we don't want to commit to something longer term, I recommend we keep doing these one-week deals."

Ken didn't know how to respond. He welcomed Arnie's support for continuing the mission program. But he was disappointed at his push for the current approach.

Arnie said, "We can make some changes, to make these more effective. And if we accept that these trips won't be perfect, at least they'll be better than nothing."

Before anyone could comment on his suggestion Lottie jumped in again. As a mental aside, Pastor Lawrence gave thanks that this was her final year on the council.

She said, "I'm also really troubled by the idea that we would work with the Catholic church in this town. I think they should get their own missionary groups."

Joachim Estes said, "But Lottie, if we don't adopt Ken's recommendation to work long-term with this village, that becomes irrelevant, doesn't it?"

Lottie replied, "Even if we don't work with this village again, I especially don't want it to be with the Catholics."

Struggling to stifle a smile, Joachim proposed that they set up a task force to see how Ken's ideas could be implemented.

They spent another eighteen minutes discussing the merits of Joachim's proposal. Lottie took four of those minutes with an obscure anecdote about a Hispanic church in town, which had established a task force to consider repaving their parking lot. In the end they couldn't afford to do that. Her only explicit point appeared to be that one Hispanic church couldn't afford to repave its parking lot. But the other council members knew there was the not-so-hidden subtext that there was something generically negative about Hispanics, and maybe their churches too.

Harry spoke vigorously, and more coherently, against the idea of the task force. "If we see no merit in setting up a long-term mission relationship, and I for one certainly don't, what the hell is the point—oops, sorry pastor—of setting up a task force to look at the idea?"

His argument won the day. The task force idea was voted down. So was Ken's main proposal.

Next the council moved on to the final agenda item, regarding the proposed gazebo in the memorial garden that the building and grounds committee recommended.

Arnie Anderson, the committee chair, said, "It will greatly beautify the garden and add to its serenity and sense of peace." Some additional landscaping would be needed and the total project, including sales tax, would come in at just under $4,400, he said.

Only two people spoke against the idea: Harry, as a matter of principle, and Joachim, who said they should commit the funds to covering the mission trip shortfall. Instead, the gazebo project was approved 10–2.

Pastor Lawrence closed the meeting in prayer.

❧

Ken went home and began scrolling through his denomination's data bank of ministerial openings.

Epilogue

NONE OF THE GROUP ever returned to San Pedro 2 or visited San Pedro 1, except Sissy Simons. She and John Braxton were married a year after the group returned home. She and John now live in nearby San Salvador, where she helps Mrs. Fernández with the used clothing store she opened in that market town.

❦

Kristen's crush on Ken ended abruptly after she returned home, when she learned that Sharon had heard from Kyra that Annabel saw Ken and Angela holding hands while strolling through Patterson Park one Saturday afternoon.

❦

Ken Barker moved to take up an assistant pastor's role in Portland, Oregon, the January after the mission trip. He remained interested in missions but his new role precluded him from leading any more trips. His relationship with Angela ended amicably and he is still single. He is in nothing that one could call a relationship right now, except for his growing affinity for Powell's Books in downtown Portland.

❦

With Ricardo's encouragement the remaining paint supplies from San Pedro 1 were sold at a nominal price to the most skilled of the day laborers who had helped paint the church. This laborer established his own painting business and now employs six painters.

❦

Ricardo left Mission Matchers to join the staff of the Raleigh church that helped the village to install its water and sewerage systems. His full-time job is to oversee the introduction of electricity over the next several years and explore the possibility of introducing a small manufacturing business in this increasingly prosperous community. Fortunately, the village is within commuting distance from his home. He and his wife had their third child, a boy, whom they named Oscar after nobody in particular.

❦

The puppets now languish in a storage unit four miles from Heidi's home, forgotten and never having seen the action and multiculturally sensitive roles that were envisaged for them.

❦

Kyra, who had a mischievous streak, signed up each of Heidi's eight puppets with Delta's mileage plan. Having obtained Heidi's email password she engaged in a protracted conversation on her behalf with Delta's SkyMiles officials, insisting on receiving credit for all the miles they'd flown. Heidi never learned who was behind the prank.

❦

Andre never did tell Priscilla the full story about his prostitution arrest. Nor did Ken. Andre told his wife that it had to do with a speeding violation. She was angry enough at all the expenses he incurred during his venture, especially the charges Avis imposed for damage to the Nissan Sentra, that she didn't pursue the matter. Crashing into the rock required considerable attention to the car's rack and pinion system, which together with the stolen hubcaps and the various dents totaled $2,468 to repair. None of it was covered by the insurance that Andre thought was part of the rental agreement; he had misunderstood the form and checked the box that waived comprehensive coverage rather than confirming it. He was so focused on his feud with Avis, which he inevitably lost, that he had no energy to take on First Church's incompetent and insolent youth pastor.

᙮

Fr. Gonzalez was killed eight months after the group left, when a truck's brakes failed and the driver lost control going down a steep hill. The truck slammed head-on into his Peugeot and he died instantly. His funeral Mass was held in San Salvador, which had the largest Catholic church in the region. Even so, it was not enough to accommodate all the mourners. Pastor Alfredo was one of half a dozen eulogists and by far the most passionate and eloquent.

᙮

Alfredo himself continued pastoring San Pedro's small evangelical church. Under his leadership the membership didn't grow much in numbers but the depth of his people's discipleship was striking. If their names earned a special notation in the Book of Life (mentioned in Revelation 3:5), he wouldn't have been surprised.

His church's soccer team continued, on average, to lose four games to the Catholics out of every five played.

᙮

Annabel and Cristina kept up a correspondence for four years, each using a friend to translate the letters they'd send. Cristina wrote about her grandchildren, who still didn't visit often enough. She always addressed Annabel as her *"querida nieta"*—"little grandchild." Annabel wrote about her graduation from high school, her time in college, and her engagement to a wonderful young man who had just graduated (from the same college) in computer science. Cristina died of cancer at the age of eighty-one, just shy of Annabel's graduation and wedding.

᙮

Bill graduated from college with a degree in sociology. He went on to get a master's in social work and now works with the homeless, in Louisville, Kentucky. He never forgot Mario and still prays for him on occasion.

᙮

The Mission Trip to San Pedro 2

The First Church council never revisited the possibility of another international mission trip. With Ken's departure, the initial support for such trips faded even further. The council decided to support only local and, after a long and contentious discussion, a handful of national missions as well. However, the banner that Pastor Alfredo and Fr. Gonzalez gave the group still hangs in the sanctuary, a reminder of the church's prior commitment to international missions.

☙❦❧

Most of the nine students in the group stayed in touch initially, especially those who kept attending First Church. But as college and, later on, jobs pulled them to other parts of the country, they grew apart. Zach and Kyrstie tried to arrange a five-year reunion of the group but it didn't work out.

Afterword and Acknowledgements

If God calls you to be a missionary, don't stoop to be a king.
—*JORDAN GROOMS*

JORDAN GROOMS' STATEMENT CAPTURES the vitally important role of missionary efforts throughout the history of the Christian church. A moment's reflection reminds us that without the vitality of mission and outreach, the church will die. Likewise, we would not have a worldwide church today were it not for the countless missionaries, beginning with Jesus' disciples and the great missionary Paul, who heeded Jesus' Great Commission to take the Good News global: "Therefore go and make disciples of all nations, baptizing them in the name of the Father and of the Son and of the Holy Spirit . . ."

The history of Christian missionaries, though, is a mixed bag. We think of the colonial era when European powers sent explorers, soldiers and missionaries into uncharted territory, claiming the land, its resources and people for King and Queen—and the souls for God. As often as not, the gospel message was inextricably interwoven with and tainted by the culture and politics of the imperial power.

Writer Lewis Hastings gives one example of how missionaries, dedicated souls from the London Missionary Society, required in their evangelism efforts in Africa that converts adopt British ways. This included clothing, especially trousers. Hastings wrote that these missionaries, "waving their braces [suspenders] like a banner, swept into the astonished kraals . . . and crammed the unwilling black limbs into those twin tubes." Unable to separate the heart of the gospel from their own cultural trappings and their assumptions about their own cultural superiority, these missionaries insisted that because this is how Christian men dressed back home, these new converts in Africa should do likewise.

Fortunately, in the past half century or so Christians in the West have begun thinking much more carefully about their approach to mission and evangelism. For example, prodigious efforts in Bible translation work have brought the gospel to indigenous communities in their own languages, laying a lasting foundation for and grounding in the Christian faith. At the same time, many missionaries and their sending agencies have distanced themselves from the old imperial or colonial approach and culturally superior mindset; they now approach their role with much greater cultural sensitivity and humility.

But not always. *The Mission Trip to San Pedro 2* is a story about one fictional mission effort that is steeped in obedience to the Great Commission but raises ongoing questions about the *how* of doing missions in the twenty-first century. Despite how some readers may respond, this story is most emphatically *not* a tale that is anti-missions. On the contrary, it is precisely because effective missionaries and missionary work are so important that I thought this story worth writing.

Finally, I need to thank several individuals who generously gave of their time in critiquing initial drafts of this story. They are Dan Burns, Mike Cardillo, Stacey Mainer, Lisa McLean, Kyle Storm, Blake Sullivan and Dan Vaughan. I am much in their debt, as well as to my son, Matthew Jackson, who tidied the final version of the manuscript with his uncanny editing and proofreading skills.

Gordon S. Jackson

CPSIA information can be obtained
at www.ICGtesting.com
Printed in the USA
FSHW020159101121